# LETTERS
# TO LITTLE
# COMRADE

**Other Titles by Dan K. Woo**

*Learning How to Love China*
*The Spirits Have Nothing to Do with Us: New Chinese Canadian Fiction*
  (editor)
*Taobao: Stories*

*Use Only in Event of Emergency*

# LETTERS TO LITTLE COMRADE

## A Guide for Girls

## Dan K. Woo

*Penalty Fine or Imprisonment for Misuse*

A Buckrider Book

This is a work of fiction. All characters, organizations, places and events portrayed are either products of the author's imagination or are used fictitiously.

Published by Buckrider Books
an imprint of Wolsak and Wynn Publishers
280 James Street North
Hamilton, ON L8R2L3
www.wolsakandwynn.ca

Editor for Buckrider Books: Paul Vermeersch | Copy editor: Ashley Hisson
Cover and interior design: Jennifer Rawlinson
Cover image: iStock.com/MorePics
Author photograph: Sam Zuo, Foto Studio
Typeset in Minion and Vendetta
Printed by Brant Service Press Ltd., Brantford, Canada

Printed on certified 100% post-consumer Rolland Enviro Paper.

10  9  8  7  6  5  4  3  2  1

The publisher gratefully acknowledges the support of the Ontario Arts Council, the Canada Council for the Arts and the Government of Canada.

**Library and Archives Canada Cataloguing in Publication**

Title: Letters to Little Comrade : a guide for girls / Dan K. Woo.
Other titles: Learning how to love China
Names: Woo, Dan K., author.
Description: Previously published under title: Learning how to love China. Toronto: Quattro Books, 2018.
Identifiers: Canadiana 20220285306 | ISBN 9781989496626 (softcover)
Classification: LCC PS8645.O472 L43 2023 | DDC C813/.6—dc23

To dad and daughter

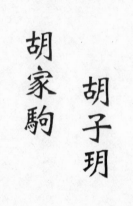

胡子玥

胡家駒

# CONTENTS

# PART THREE

# PART FOUR

# PART FIVE

# DISCLAIMER

This material is meant for nationals of the People's Republic of Qina. Please be advised this guide does not purport to contain actionable information. If your life is in immediate jeopardy, or you have suicidal thoughts, contact your nearest health care provider or dial 110 for emergency services.

Please note this book is produced by the Qinese Bureau of Public Affairs and is not intended for sale or distribution outside Mainland Qina.

# PART ONE

# I. KEEP CALM,
# THERE IS HOPE

Thank you for purchasing *Letters to Little Comrade: A Guide for Girls*. Good for you!

This collection of letters will help you become a responsible citizen. It will show you how to let go of unpatriotic thinking. Read it with an open mind. It may change your life and start you on your road to inner peace and recovery.

Other materials previously released by the Qinese Bureau of Public Affairs include *Understanding Tax Code for Simpletons*, *Purchasing a Home Responsibly* and *Relocating to Tibet/Xinjiang New Territory*. You may find a complete listing at www.zgbmaiguo.cn. All these guides are helpful in a manner similar to this guide.

Before you begin, select a country that will serve as your ideal living destination. A place where you want more than anything to move to, to live, to work, to raise your family. Do not be fearful, everyone has a secret dream. It can be anywhere in the world, for example, Australia, Italy, France or Canada. For the purposes of this book, you will be using a country called "America."

This "America" is on the North American continent approximately eleven thousand kilometres from your current location. The people there look different from you and they speak a language that is difficult if not impossible for us Qinese to master. Most likely you have heard about this "America" on QQ Tencent news channel or from idle gossip with coworkers. It's a place rumoured to have an endless amount of clear blue skies, beautiful lakes, pristine forests, clean friendly cities and handsome men. You've heard that if only you can get there, all your problems will be solved. All of this may very well be true, but there is no need to panic.

Right now, "America" seems like the perfect place to be, doesn't it? Perhaps you just came off your shift. You must be exhausted, unhappy, generally dissatisfied with your surroundings, your employer and maybe even, worst of all, your government. You feel the irresistible urge to blame others for your woes. Do not worry, those feelings are natural.

You're walking back along the main road, along the six-lane bridge, along with thousands of your factory coworkers. A veritable sea of human beings, all wearing the same dark green uniform, moving in opposing currents. One shift of workers is heading east, the other shift is going west. Just like a microcosm of the globe. There're so many of you that the six-lane bridge has been permanently retrofitted with a large fence down the middle to accommodate the bustling flow.

The outdoor entrance to the workers' dormitory compound is protected by twenty revolving turnstiles, each equipped with hi-tech facial recognition and ID scanner. Go ahead and take a moment to appreciate the cutting-edge, nationally made technology.

Guards are posted on the left, and a police barracks is on the right. On the opposing side of the boulevard hundreds of workers buzz and flit like insects feeding on a seemingly endless row of food stalls. The sky is dark. The night shift workers are heading out as you stand there lost in contemplation.

You're thinking to yourself, anchored to the ground as you are, in this choppy ocean of dark green outfits, that everyone looks the same, whether they are young or old, female or male. All of you are the same. So what makes you different? What is wrong with you?

The only difference is that you feel overwhelmed by the work. You do not feel like a bad egg, but maybe you are after all. You want to move to a nicer place like this "America" you have heard so much about. Maybe it is a new idea that you hatched in recent days. Or maybe you have always felt this way, ever since you were a baby girl in your father's village, before you got a job at the factory in the big city. Do not fret, this book can help you overcome that tiresome and unwanted desire. This simple collection of letters is your ticket to boosting self-confidence and escaping your unfortunate state of mind. So keep reading, dear Little Comrade.

# II. KNOW WHERE
# YOU ARE

It is always better to face the facts. Look around. In front of the turnstiles, what do you see?

You see the uneven, unfinished boulevard where workers mingle and eat. You see motorbike taxis driving back and forth. Some of these big loud bikes are covered with flashing multicoloured lights, decorated garishly. The operators honk and try to pick up fares. As workers traverse the wide boulevard over to the food stalls, they are liable to be run over by one of these muscular vehicles roaring at full speed in the dark. Be careful as you cross to get some food.

Whichever direction you turn, a motorbike is there honking at you to get your attention, offering to drive you wherever you want. If only he could drive you to "America" you would gladly hop on the back seat. Unfortunately for you, it cannot be. You are where you are.

The tooting of bullhorns from merchants' carts and food vendors hawking their goods make your eardrums hurt. The place is lively and brimming with excitement. Ask yourself, are you sure you want to leave such a noisy, high-energy environment?

Just remember, you've made friends here among your bunkmates and coworkers. And isn't it the case that a good-looking young man from the Quality Assurance Department has expressed a romantic interest in you? You may have suspected it before, since every time he visits the assembly line where you work, he makes eyes at you. Who knows, perhaps he will ask for your WeChat contact next time you see him.

True, the assembly line is exhausting. You're tired of working six days a week, having only Sundays off every month. The pay is so little – 2,500 yuan a month. At twelve hours a day, six days a week, that's around eight yuan an hour. If you went to "America" and exchanged your hard-earned hourly wage for an American "buck," you would not have enough to buy half a bus token. How embarrassing! And what's more, you don't want to live in a cramped dorm room with seven others, even if they are your friends, which you really doubt.

You may also be thinking to yourself that the air quality is terrible. The pollution from the nearby factories makes your head hurt, and you get so much pressure from your boss to hurry up production on the line. It's not a place for anyone to live, let alone a sensitive, intelligent young woman like you.

With all these troubles on your mind, this is a good time to pause and reflect on what your parents said to you when you left home, and to reflect on the filial duties every child has.

True, you are not a son. But being a female does not excuse you from family obligations to your parents.

In fact, as a daughter, you are in even greater debt to your parents.

You were born first and you failed to be a son, and good governmental policy allowed them to try again, until they succeeded. But you were already born, you were a mistake, and yet they had the decency to raise you all those years from infancy to adulthood. All for what? At least a son can bring respect to his parents. He can carry on the family name, be successful in business, create wealth, make money. He can give never-ending face to his father and mother by virtue of his mere existence. You, on the other hand . . .

It's your responsibility to send money back to them. You can't just quit the job at the factory, because where will you get money? It's shameful for a daughter who has already taken so much from her parents since birth to ask for more. No one is so shameless.

# III. BE HAPPY
# WHERE YOU ARE

For the time being, factory life makes you miserable, and yet you don't want to return to your hometown and submit to the wishes of your parents. What can you do?

Think. Who will give you a job if not the factory? The factory doesn't pay well, but at least it's honest work. There aren't too many other options, are there? Restaurant, shop, hair salon – are any of these better or worse than the factory? You can decide, it's up to you. You can have as much freedom as you like here, just as much as in "America."

But at the moment your stomach is growling, you are hungry. Look around. Food stalls are arranged in a long line, one pressed up against the next, each no more than two arm spans wide. If you go around the back there are more options. How can you not be satisfied with all the choices you have? Do you really think you would prefer the strange, unappetizing foodstuffs they have in "America"?

Here sits a steamed dumpling stand, there a noodle stand. Cold cuts and assortments abound farther down. Fried rice and noodles everywhere, your favourite. Soybean drink stand, bean curd soup stand, hot sour skewer stand, BBQ stand, the egg and meat patty stand and rice gruel stand with sixteen different kinds of rice gruel in paper cups wrapped with plastic. Brown bean, red bean, green bean, eight precious bean, pumpkin flavour, squash – the list is satisfyingly long.

Maybe to you it all tastes like slop. But at least it gives you strength to do your job and get paid. Besides, no one likes a complainer, it decreases production and morale. Always try to look on the bright side, especially when others are nearby.

There're multiples of each food stand, so you don't need to walk far to collect your nourishment. Check out the new sushi stand, it's Taiwan Sushi. Patronize it. They will become dependent on your money and that is a good thing. Without you, they will not be able to survive for even one day. Even if it tastes bad, even if it's fake Taiwan Sushi and there's corn and sickly sweet white salad dressing mushed into the rice, try it. Their menu is laminated and professional looking.

The breakfast dumpling stand is open night and day, so it's available to both shifts of workers. The basket steamers hold delectable delicacies. Purple rice pudding triangles, lotus leaf zongzi festival dumplings, sweet yellow cornbread, baozi full of pork or bok choy and succulent morsels of mushroom, carrot and bean sprout vermicelli. What you eat is your choice. Take comfort knowing you are in control.

The line of food stalls is to the left of the dormitory turnstile entrance. Directly in front of the entrance hundreds of coworkers mill and mix. A TV is blaring on the makeshift space. Every night, people watch, fixated on the screen. Whatever show happens to be playing – whether it is classic opera, kung fu, sports – workers will stand for hours, mesmerized by the intoxicating programming.

On the dusty walkway beyond, a group of men play with a couple of arcade machines. They put coins into the machines and operate toy grappling hooks like they are trying to grab stuffed bears. But inside these machines are heaps of unopened cigarette packs. How fun! If you have a coin, you can try too.

Other workers line up at the Bank of Qina ATM, eager to check their bank balances, no doubt. Everything everywhere is plastered with cheap mono-coloured ads the size of business cards, but even this litter and defacement of private and public property infuses the dreary scene with a rainbow-like feel akin to musical theatre.

To the right side, follow the wide boulevard. Nicer restaurants are over this way. Here, workers are happy to spend their hard-earned cash for better food. They sit patiently, elbows on the tables. Though the interior lights are hardly on, and the air is nearly unbreathable due to clouds of cooking fumes and second-hand smoke, a respectable family atmosphere is noticeable. Order what you wish in comfort, such as rice topped with freshly cooked pork.

Beyond that, a cluster of ad hoc factory recruitment shanties set up by shady middlemen occupies the grounds, ready to grab any unsuspecting but able-bodied bystander. They have their billboards out, listing the jobs open. The ads entice people by posting excellent paying jobs. You, obviously, can't get these jobs due to your lack of education, your poor manners and your unwanted gender. But don't feel glum. Rest assured, most of those high-paying jobs are just for show, they serve only to lure people in.

Outside, on an adjoining road used little by public traffic, there're some fruit carts. Also, knickknack stands that sell blankets, mats, cheap household items of the variety itinerant workers may desire.

You haven't eaten fruit for a while, so you decide to buy fruit. You can choose what fruit you want to buy. You like apples, so that's what you get. But, wait a minute, you think the apples are too expensive. Maybe in a few months they'll be cheaper. You decide to wait until then.

The yam seller is present, roasting his yams in an old oil drum. Even though they're expensive, you crave a juicy, hot, freshly baked yam. It's time for you to make a decision. You count your money. Are you sure you don't want to send money home to your ailing parents instead?

You have to eat; your stomach is grumbling. Splurge and buy the smallest one, why not? Go ahead, no one is looking. It tastes so good and sweet.

With your mouth full, looking around greedily, you see the tofu seller. He's got a rectangular hot plate on his cart and wide slabs of tofu, cut up and sizzling under onions and spices and peppers.

"Only five yuan for a double serving!" says the hawker. As you lick your lips in gluttonous desire, you hear someone calling your name, it stands out from the honking of the motorbikes and the noisy bedlam around you. You see your best friend and bunkmate Little Bo Bo.

# IV. EXERCISE IS HEALTHY FOR THE SPIRIT

Bo Bo is a pretty, nimble young woman with a pale, heart-shaped face. You and Bo Bo were born in the same year, under the Ox. But you are her elder by a month, and she looks up to you. When fellow comrades look up to you, you have an extra duty and burden to act morally and to work hard, never forget that.

Before you know it, Bo Bo has you by the arm, chattering about her boyfriend. As she talks, she buys pan-fried tofu squares and some kebabs. She's recounting her birthday, two nights ago, when she and her boyfriend, also a coworker at the factory, went to La Viva, a rundown little hotel squeezed next to a mobile phone store.

In front of the hotel is where you're standing now, on the opposite side of the street from the tofu seller. La Viva is part of a plaza that exists solely, as if by divine city planning, for the factory workers.

The windows of La Viva are tinted – it's a sleazy place to be sure. But it serves its purpose, especially on weekends when new couples are in need of a private setting where they can satiate their primitive urges. Obviously, the worker dormitories, which guard strictly against gender mixing, similar to university campuses across the country, are not an option for them.

Near the entrance to La Viva is an industrial-sized subwoofer, planted on the parking lot grounds, courtesy of the mobile phone store. All through the evening it blasts bombastic techno music that can be heard for a mile in every direction, perhaps in an effort to drown out the mysterious squeals that emit from the neighbouring hotel. Needless to say, this is as fine a place as any for an evening stroll.

"Big sister," Bo Bo teases, "when are you going to get a boyfriend?"

A hard question to answer. You want to appear "cool" in front of your bunkmate.

"Soon," you say, as you smooth your hair back with one hand.

You've never had a boyfriend, and you're not sure what it entails. But there's that boy from the Quality Assurance Department who makes eyes at you, remember? QAD Boy, or Q for short, that's your nickname for him. Q drops by your section once a week on an errand, and each time he visits, you feel his presence. So, in a way, you are not lying. Perhaps you really will have a boyfriend soon. Lucky you!

Inside the plaza, in one corner, opposite the outdoor billiards tables where trendy-looking, young male workers off work shoot pool, you stand by a roller rink.

About a hundred skaters move before you in a quixotic dance, like so many excited particles of energy. You've only been skating once or twice before and you don't like sports. But Bo Bo likes skating with her boyfriend, and she wants to practise.

"Come on, sis," says Bo Bo. "I learned how to skate backwards. Let me show you. My treat!"

The rink is recklessly overcrowded. There are no rules, it is a free-for-all. Helmetless roller skaters on the outer circle whirl by so fast they are like evil kamikaze pilots looking for a helpless target. They twirl, spin, flip in complete disregard for their surroundings. Other less adept skaters form chains, holding hands in solidarity, bringing to mind our country's glorious revolutionary past.

You don't really want to skate, you're tired. Nevertheless, Bo Bo pulls you around the rink to where the tickets are sold. It is an open-air arena, only covered over top; it's lit up and it's nighttime. The loud music is exciting and energizes everyone but you. Perhaps you are tired because you are over-worked in the factory.

The shops that flank the roller rink are either closed or abandoned. They cannot compete with the excitement of the rink. Poor shops! The only two that still try are the hair salon and the web cafe, which are up a flight of metal stairs on the second-floor balcony.

The skates hurt your feet. They stink and haven't been deodorized once in the five years they have been in commission. Admittedly, deodorizing is not a "thing" in this country, as it may be in "America." Nevertheless, this fails to interest you.

Put on the skates, wiggle your toes. Next thing you know Bo Bo is pulling you along. How does it feel? No doubt roller-skating can provide the same cheap thrill whether you are in your own country, Qina, or far far away in that underpopulated and sparse wasteland called "America."

Bo Bo is getting really good at roller-skating, having had so much practice recently with her handsome young boyfriend. She doesn't look awkward like you, with your arms flailing wildly every other second to keep you from falling over. You may be a menace to yourself and the skaters around you, but it fails to prevent you from trying to have fun. If only you were so devoted to improving your work ethic at the factory, and to satisfying your parents' demands.

Bo Bo has more or less mastered the art of stopping, though her ankles are crooked and her posture is cringeworthy. Her attempts are admirable, as are yours.

All you can do is try to keep from colliding with one of these roller-skating daredevils. Everyone on the rink seems to be joyfully suicidal. Bo Bo isn't fearful for her own safety; she's having the time of her life. But you are quite afraid.

Over on the far side of the rink a girl has "wiped out." A slick young guy with a perfect hairdo flying on his wheels crashed into her and elbowed her in the neck. Oh well, what's done is done. He continues on his way. The injured party sits in a mangled heap, like the victim of a freak car accident. Her hair is streaked over her face, her limbs jut out at unreal angles. No one comes to her aid, not even the two rink staff members who are busy taking money and selling more tickets. Skate at your own peril, dear Little Comrade.

The slick, coiffured skater is still skating. He does an airborne twirl like he's in the Beijing Olympics. Slowly the injured woman crawls to safety. By the rails, she clutches her head with one hand and her stomach with the other, sobbing. Don't worry, no need to tend to her. Just like our country fighting tooth and nail against Nationalist and Imperialist collaborators, it's a blood sport. Everyone for herself.

In the meantime, Bo Bo has skated out in front of you. She has little trouble achieving her desired velocity. Whereas you are stuck at a glacial pace. Despite the fact that you make slow progress in the net distance you cover, your feet slip and zigzag about at almost comically fast speeds.

Then, unwittingly, you edge into a wrong lane, an unspoken path that has no markings. A speed demon comes at you and ducks out of the way just in the nick of time. Behind him is another, and another, in rapid succession, like bullets. You dodge one, but for the second, you hurl yourself toward the side of the rink, hoping to catch yourself on the rail.

Someone grabs a hold of you. You cannot see who it is, because your eyes are closed. You think you might be dead.

But you are not dead, and there is no point in keeping your eyes closed. You blink twice and see Q. He has a firm grip on your upper arm, propping you up. He is the young man from the Quality Assurance Department located in Area 2, across the street from you, who comes to your Section 4 assembly line on occasion to complete a client's request.

"What's the matter?" you say indignantly, flushing from head to toe. "Let go of me."

"Hey," he says, "I thought you were falling over."

"Well, I wasn't." You want to thank him, but you can feel people's eyeballs watching you. Don't give others the wrong impression. Don't make a spectacle out of yourself. Improper relations between a young man and a young woman can spell disaster for all involved, especially if they're coworkers.

There're so many people leaning on the rails, all sorts of guys and girls, watching your every movement, speculating what will happen, if you will swoon and fall in love right there, just like in a romantic film. You don't want them to think you are a "little missy," a young woman with loose morals, unworthy of sleeping in her own parents' house.

"Don't I know you from somewhere?" he says. He is smoking, but perhaps spurred by some momentary lapse of reason, looking into your eyes, he stubs out his cigarette.

"No, I don't think so."

You pull yourself along the rail. Q is talking to you, yet you ignore him. He's on the other side of the rail, wearing ordinary shoes. He follows you. "I like watching the rink; I come here once or twice a week. My friends are grabbing something to eat, but I thought I'd keep watching because I saw you. I've never seen you skate before, so I was surprised."

"Well, I do, I skate a lot, can't you tell? Anyway, I'm with my friend. Goodbye!"

"Wait a minute," he says, "let me add your WeChat, okay? We can have a bite to eat some time."

"I don't add strangers," you say. "There's too many good-for-nothings doing mischief online. I don't want to get scammed."

"I'm not a scammer, I work at the factory just like you. I've seen you on the line. Section four, right?"

The fact that he knows your section number makes your heart quicken. You're thinking, just for a moment, whether or not to give him your WeChat ID, that unique identifier that is so suddenly, miraculously valuable.

You have the freedom to choose. But, for some reason, it doesn't feel like it's your choice. He lingers there, a hint of impatience, of hidden violence. He isn't willing to go away unless you tell him what he wants to know. Does it make you feel flattered?

Quick, think! Bo Bo will see you any minute. If and when that happens, you won't have a chance to give it to him, it'll be too embarrassing in front of a friend. The situation would be unbearable. Make a spur of the moment decision. Hurry, before it's too late! In an uncharacteristic burst of courage, you decide to give him your WeChat, if only, you console yourself, to get rid of him.

You take out your phone, feeling more confident, more reassured in the physical world with it in your hand. But it is old and the screen is cracked. You try to hide your embarrassment. His phone is nicer, newer, more expensive than yours. But at least his phone isn't an iPhone, which makes you feel a bit better.

"What department are you in?" you ask him.

"I'm a quality control engineer," says Q.

"Oh yeah? How much do you make?"

"Four thousand three hundred yuan." He shrugs.

The figure is astronomical compared to your paltry monthly salary of 2,500. But jealousy among coworkers is bad for factory production. Try to suppress your immature feelings. You try hard to hide the jealousy, but your face twitches. Calm down, Little Comrade. Know that he's exaggerating. It's nothing more than a misguided attempt to impress the girl he wants.

As you battle the mental anguish in your mind, he seizes the opportunity. He scans the QR barcode on your phone display. On the outside, the smooth operator is "cool as a cucumber." But on the inside Q is smiling, he's triumphant. He has taken what he wanted. Just in time too. Out of the corner of your eye you see Bo Bo. Feeling hot all over, you quickly hurry away from Q.

"Who was that?" Bo Bo asks.

"Nobody, just some weirdo. Come on, I'm tired, let's go home."

# V. BE REALISTIC, DON'T DAYDREAM

Everyone daydreams on occasion, it's okay. But for most people, they fantasize about succeeding in work, being elevated to a higher position of respect in our society, making some contribution that will help their fellow citizens.

For you, by contrast, it's dreaming about this seemingly fictitious place, "America." You dream about the president of "America," a man rumoured to be so handsome his movie star looks are blinding. You even invent a name for this imaginary fellow. You call him "Ryan Reynolds," a preposterous jumble of letters and sounds so improbable and difficult to pronounce that it delights you. Finally, to top it all off, you install what you suppose is a photo of him on your phone, staring at it for hours on end, with a sappy, dopey-eyed expression on your face.

Instead, you should be standing in front of the mirror and studying what you see. Time has not been kind to you. The twenty-odd years you have spent on this planet have been cruel to your beauty. Your parents are right. Soon, suitors once desperate to marry you will scoff when you knock on their doors. You must act quickly.

You are in your dorm room, and it is dark outside. Like you, your bunkmates go to sleep late, lying on their beds, playing on their phones. The beds are made of metal frames with hard matchwood boards. The bedrolls and blankets are owned by each individual worker. Yours is thin, cheap material, but you're used to it.

The electricity to the harsh fluorescent ceiling lights cuts out precisely at 11:00 p.m. every night. The room lights are off now. You are on your side, stretched out on the upper bunk. You can see Bo Bo's face across from you, glowing from the candescence of her smartphone. She's chatting with her beloved boyfriend on WeChat. Feeling a little jealous, you look at your own phone. You're surprised to see a new conversation notification blinking, waiting for you to open it.

The message is from Q, the young man from the Quality Assurance Department.

All it contains is a smiley face and a "What's up?" A succinct enough communication, but hardly a model example of our country's six-decade-long literacy struggle.

You were daydreaming earlier about "America," your mind lost in a foggy swamp of nonsensical images. Having something to do, your attention focuses like a laser beam. You prop yourself up on one elbow, eager to make a witty response.

"Nothing, you?" You tap out the Pinyin, selecting the characters as they appear. It's easy to write on your phone, thanks to the innovations of your fellow citizens. You are such a fast typist that the characters flash on the screen like you are playing Whac-A-Mole, a popular children's game in "America."

The series of emoticons that subsequently passes between you and Q is neither interesting nor of much literary value. But the personal excitement and entertainment you derive is real. After half an hour of idle banter, mediocre jokes and beer bar philosophy, you agree to meet Q after work the following day.

This night you rest fitfully, possibly because you feel your date with Q is a betrayal of the impossibly named "Ryan Reynolds." When you wake up late, the communal bathroom is already crowded. As punishment for your tardiness, you have no choice but to fix yourself up using the plastic-framed mirror bought in a spending spree one day last year from the knickknack stand.

As you comb your hair, it may serve you well to recall your working conditions, to help you mentally prepare for the day so you can be a better "worker bee."

# VI. SEEK TRUTH
# FROM FACTS

To begin with, the factory workers' residential compound where you live, known casually as B Dorm, holds the most common, lowest paid workers. The facility has eight cube-like structures, each housing over a thousand workers. Each worker pays 120 yuan/month out of their salary for their bunk. Seven of these structures house the male workers, and the leftover one is for the women. Line workers like you live eight to a room, and occupy floors one to five, eight to twelve. The office workers, who are better paid, live six to a room, and take floors six and seven. This is where Q, for example, lives in one of the seven male dorms, on either the sixth or seventh floor.

A Dorm, the other worker residence compound, sits just outside of the periphery of the industrial zone, and holds the rest of the female workers, along with some of the company's leaders and Taiwanese managers. Aside from having slightly better conditions, A Dorm is also closer to the downtown area. In total, A Dorm and B Dorm combined have a fluctuating population of around twenty thousand workers.

The company you work for is a minor player in the industry, hardly noticeable. It is not like Foxconn, the well-known maker of Apple iPhones, located a few kilometres to the east of you, in their own separate industrial community. But still, you should feel proud of where you work. Each factory, no matter how small, no matter how unknown, contributes in some way to the overall health of the economy.

To be clear, the factory where you work doesn't actually manufacture anything, strictly speaking. What the factory does do, and by extension you and your coworkers, is assemble premade parts into computers and other computer hardware for different clients, according to client specifications. There are clients from all over the world, even from your beloved "America." Dell, Acer, Hongji and a whole host of others. All of these companies come to our country because they know that we have the most efficient, best manufacturing process on the planet. As a worker, no matter how low your salary, or how minuscule your contribution, you can feel productive knowing you are part of this successful system.

Indeed, helping make so many electronics without even a recognizable brand name, the factory is like the wizard behind the curtain in that story popular in "America," *The Wizard of Oz*, pulling the levers and gears, while unseen by the public.

If you feel depressed, unmotivated while you work, think of yourself as that wizard. You are in control. You control the fate and destiny of the world's supply of electronics. Good work, Little Comrade! Together our country will rise above others.

But here you are, thinking of "America" once more. Just the mere mention of anything "American" turns your mind into jelly. For the weaker comrades, if it sometimes helps to visualize a symbol of hope, something to help you get through the day, that can be permitted on occasion. You probably would enjoy imagining the star-and-striped banner, the national symbol of "America," or perhaps an "American football." Mix it up. It doesn't always have to be that unrealistically handsome president Mr. "Reynolds." Perhaps, you are thinking, when you get to "America" you'll meet him and shake his hand, and he'll kiss you.

Have you stopped to consider that the face etched in your mind is possibly nothing more than a propaganda tool for the country's fledgling tourism industry? Oh, what a naive little girl you are!

Stop studying his face on your phone. Instead, look at yourself in the mirror. The colour, the texture, the dullness – doesn't it surprise you? Remember what you see.

Outside the window, it's sunny out. You can't see the sun because of the fog that's always in the sky, but the fog, or smog, whatever they call it, is illuminated; it's a dust cloud that transmits light. The radiance is charming in its own right. Do not dismiss its beauty merely because it is the combination of depleted ozone and toxic pollution. Enjoy the white sky, that subtle gradient of mustard yellow to grey, with hints and splashes of peach-red.

# VII. OBEY YOUR ELDERS

Off to work you go. All day you work like all your friends and coworkers, obedient comrades who are doing their patriotic duty and being paid well enough to purchase adequate sustenance. All day long and into the evening, day after day, the days blur together. Be careful, do not "zone out" as you assemble the computers. Pay attention! Do not bring disgrace upon our nation.

Sure, the work may be mindless, but such factory work exists everywhere in the world. Most people don't mind the work and can even be cheerful about it. But to you, Little Comrade, it feels worse, more soul-crushing, because you, more than others, are rebellious by nature.

When you come in and out of Area 3, the diligent security guards check you in the metal detector for metallic objects. You are free to bring as many electronic gadgets as you want into the compound – USB keys, your own keyboards, mouse, laptops, if you so desire. But if you wish to bring them back out, you will discover to your dismay that you cannot. The items now belong for all eternity to the factory. Silly you, you should have read the workers' preparatory handout.

Just like that, the day is over. See, factory life is not too hard. They have a popular saying in "America": "Time flies when you're having fun." So, after all, there is some wisdom to be gleaned from that mushy part of the planet. You see the clock, your time is up, you punch out your shift, it's a breeze. Why not spend your whole life here?

On your leisurely evening stroll back to your dormitory, your phone rings. The screen flashes – it's your mother.

"Daughter," she says in a shrill voice. "Daughter?"

"Hello, Mama," you say. "Hello, Mama!" Repeatedly you shout into the phone. She cannot hear you; reception is poor. Perhaps it is the crack on your phone's screen.

When communication resumes your mother is in the midst of an interrogation.

"What are you doing?" she says. "What are you eating? Are you off work?" A dozen questions are flung at you before you can answer the first. "You should come home," she says. "Third Auntie's neighbour has a son. We want you to meet him."

"I don't want to," you say.

Unfortunately, you should have said, "Yes, of course, Mama." But such lessons as these you ignored many years ago, and there is no reason to expect you to heed them now. Fine, you must suffer the consequences of your selfish, childish backtalk. Your mother explodes in a fit of self-pity and frustration. Who can blame her for losing patience with an ungrateful daughter?

"What's the point of just wasting time in the city?" she wails. "What are you accomplishing in the factory? Don't be such a stupid girl. Hurry up and come home. Why are you doing this to me? Don't always think only about yourself. Do what's best for everyone." Shouldn't you respect her wishes? She is your mother after all. But no, that would be the decent thing to do, and you, of course, are above doing the decent thing.

Any other mother would long have given up on you, yet here you are, hardly grateful to her for such never-ending tender, motherly affection. It may be difficult for you to listen to your mother's advice, but try. If not for the sake of her health, then for our country.

The conversation proceeds in a similar, repetitive manner over the next ten minutes as you plod to your dorm. Your mother threatens to put your father on the phone. She extorts a promise from you that you will visit at the next possible opportunity. Please listen to her and you will get better.

Groups of workers are walking home, many individually. Like you the others are in a state of flux, coming or going, waiting to progress to the next stage in their adult lives, but currently stuck where they are, unable to decide what to do next. Your mother is right, factory life is not for you. Go on home, Little Comrade. Live comfortably as a housewife. By doing so, you are still serving the country well and no one will look down on you for it.

"I have to eat now, Mama," you say, making up an excuse to get off the phone. "And my stomach hurts."

Your stomach indeed does hurt, you just started noticing. You don't know if it was hurting before, or if it started hurting because that's what you told your mother. Be careful, because lies can turn into truth.

You hang up the phone. Before you can slip it into your pocket, it chirps. It's a message from your new "flame," Q.

He's waiting for you by the soy milk stand. Miraculously your tummy hurts no more. You tell him you have to go up to your dorm and change out of your factory uniform first.

While you change, all the words that your mother said to you just now bounce about in your head. Instead of heeding her advice, you redouble your efforts to enjoy yourself while you have this limited amount of freedom left. You decide to make the most of your numbered days.

"I will listen to my mother, but first," you say to yourself, "before I give up my dreams, I'll have some fun. Some fun before I get married and live a quiet life."

So, having abandoned yourself to this frivolous way of thinking, you become determined to accept Q's romantic overtures. There really is no winning with you, dear Little Comrade.

# VIII. FIND ROMANCE WHEN THE TIME IS RIGHT

When you meet Q, he's sipping on a disposable cup of soy milk. He offers to buy you one, but, not wanting to appear greedy before him, you politely decline. He compliments you on your fashion sense. This is the first time he has seen you out of uniform, evidently. In embarrassment, you avoid his eyes. But when you have a chance, you study his face.

In the slanting, dying sunlight, he looks so different, older than you previously thought. But age makes men mature, wise, honourable. Q also has numerous pockmarks around his jawline, evidence of a childhood infection or repeated acne outbreaks. His teeth are stained from smoking. Still, moved by your irrational desire to rebel against parental authority, you find yourself attracted to him.

Q wants to take you to see a movie. You're glad you changed out of your work uniform, because seeing a movie means exiting the industrial zone, to gather, socialize, collect with normal human beings.

The idea sounds excellent, since you haven't gone to the movie theatre for a long time. Before, you thought it was a waste of money. For one, the tickets are always so expensive. Upwards of twenty yuan, for one seat, without refreshments even. Why pay when you can just stream movies onto your phone? But now that a boy is taking you, it's a luxury you feel you might get used to.

There's a new movie out. A romantic comedy starring Daniel Wu, the well-known Qinese American actor. You hope that by watching the movie, not only will you get pleasure in seeing his pretty face, you might learn something more about this elusive "America." But, Little Comrade, please remember as you watch it that Daniel Wu is as much Qinese, if not more so, as he is "American." That is something to consider when you are ogling him.

Q doesn't share your enthusiasm for Daniel Wu. Originally, he wanted to see a Hong Kong movie about corrupt police officers. In the end, however, he graciously submits to your request. A Hollywood movie is playing, but both of you avoid such films. Perhaps this is due to minor errors in the subtitle translation, or the bizarre cultural references. Or perhaps it's something else having to do with America's inflated sense of self-worth that seems to seep into every movie they make, which ruins what otherwise might be an enjoyable experience.

Anyway, you have Daniel Wu so you don't need Hollywood. Just thinking of Daniel Wu almost makes you forget about his fellow countryman, that other hunky princeling, "Mr. Reynolds." Already you can feel your heart thumping, and you start to feel a tingly hormonal excitement between your legs that you don't understand.

To the movie theatre then. The closest one is in the RT-Mart Mall, just a fifteen-minute bus ride from where you are. The theatre in this mall, though it is old and the screens are of inferior quality, is closer than the ones downtown, and will save you time.

How will you get there? Normally you worry about these things, but Q is here. Sit back, let the man make the decisions. You can relax and rest assured that all will proceed smoothly.

Q doesn't take you by the hand, but you walk together. Like two awkward newlyweds who have just met each other, you make your way to the bus stop by the street. A row of licensed taxis as well as motorbikes and mini-taxis wait. The mini-taxis are motorbikes that have a makeshift cart fixed on the rear.

Q wants to impress you with a taxi ride, understandable given that you're on a first date. But a taxi to the RT-Mart Mall will run up the meter. You feel him hesitating, unsure what to do.

In order to help him save face, you say, "Let's take the bus, it'll be more fun."

A charitable act on your part, well done, Little Comrade. For his part, Q keeps up his charade. He acts "cool." He shrugs. "Okay." Anyway, he can have a smoke while you wait with him.

So, with your new "bae," you wait. The crowd becomes larger and larger. The bus is always delayed, because the factory is so isolated. First there's ten, then twenty, then thirty passengers, waiting under, beside, in front of and around the shelter. They're your neighbours in the dorm, they're your coworkers in the factory, on your assembly line. Take a look around. Do you recognize any of them?

They look young, just like you. They look scrubby, even though they've put on their best outfits to go to town. The men have hard, mean expressions on their faces. They don't smile, they look like street toughs, out to pick a fight. In reality, they're harmless workers who assemble computers day and night, computers that are shipped all over the world, and no doubt to every city, town and village in "America." At night they eat, smoke, drink and chat with friends. They don't do drugs, there's no bad mischief in an industrial quarter. There's not even petty crime, security is so tight. Nobody has time for mischief, everyone is working, trying to be a responsible comrade. Everyone is trying to buy an iPhone, trying to take a girl out to a movie, trying to get married, trying to send money home to parents.

Besides, the police barracks is right at the entrance of the workers' dormitory compound. There are security guards posted at each of the entrances. But the guards are relaxed. They don't heed the chaotic hurricane of human activity. The police would just get in the way, the police would slow down production and they're there to do just the opposite. Everyone knows how to behave; everyone is trying to get ahead. That is the revolutionary way. All together, like a hive mind, the entire country heaves forward in lockstep with this purpose. The political and business elite are only there to serve, to make the country progress harmoniously. You, too, dear Little Comrade, are part of this, even though you might not be aware that it's affecting your body, your spirit, your entire destiny.

As you stand on the bus, crowded with the other factory workers, take a moment to reflect on this, your destiny.

You're the eldest child, the daughter, born under the one-child policy. So, that's to say, you're the product of a failed pregnancy. Remember your destiny. Make it up to your parents, honour their sacrifice. Return the debt you owe them for raising you so selflessly. But wait, here you are gallivanting through the night with a boy you hardly know, going to sit in a dark room to watch what will likely be suggestive images on the "silver screen." While poor mother and father toil at home, no less, to save and scrounge every coin. What an ungrateful child, flouting destiny, flouting your filial responsibilities!

The guilt, the pain, makes your chest hurt. Your eyes well up with tears of remorse. Hold that feeling close to you. Let that feeling linger, Little Comrade, try to cherish that beautiful feeling.

Unfortunately, the moment doesn't last. The effects wear off in the hubbub of life. Q is looking over at you, making eyes. You catch him in the act.

At that very moment, Q was relishing the curve of your nose, the little dimples in your cheeks, your unusually exquisite jawbone, the five near-invisible freckles under your left eye. Embarrassed at being caught by you, he averts his gaze down.

In your momentary privacy, you allow yourself a smile. You're buoyed in your spirit. Your self-worth has risen, like a single drop of water added to a pond.

A forward-facing seat is free. Go ahead, sit down. There are only young people here, and you are all equal. No one is more or less entitled to that seat.

Q is obscured by the intervening body of a worker who is still wearing his dark green uniform. You look out the window. Sundown has not yet come. The slanting rays are still lighting up the air, the sun's beams diffuse through the blanket of picturesque smog.

Toward evening on a good clear day, just at this time, if you look way up to the apex of the sky, you can see the fog or smog or whatever it is clearing at the very top. You can see a patch of faint blue sky the size of your thumb. Look closely, you will see it. If you look down just slightly, anywhere slightly lower than the apex, the blue melds into white haze. This is not a big city, it's not a dirty city, it's one of the cleanest cities and most well-kept cities in the country. Looking at this beautiful scenery, you imagine, if all of "America" looks this nice, you'll be happy.

# IX. ENJOY
# COMMERCIAL ACTIVITY

The bus you're on, city public bus 210B, pulls with some effort along the mostly empty factory roads until it reaches the large foreboding gate that separates definitively, like a guillotine through which the road and its traffic must pass, the industrial area from the rest of the city. Here, at an enormous intersection so big it could have been constructed with intergalactic alien vessels in mind, the public bus motors through after waiting at a red light.

You are out of the industrial zone now, officially. Around, on the streets, the evening nightlife abounds. People getting off work, stopping at the mall, collecting around bus stations, going to restaurants. All of this excitement lasts until around 8:30 p.m. By nine, nine thirty at the latest, the streets are thankfully clear. The city's public buses, in collaboration with careful policy planners and the business leaders, end their day. The comrades have no choice but to return to their bunks and rest so that they will have energy for the coming workday. Luckily, this routine is well entrenched, so that technological developments like DiDi car will do little to disrupt it. Everything runs so smoothly our citizens don't even notice. It is as if a divine, benevolent power rules the entire world, no matter which way they turn, no matter how far they may travel.

Bus 210B drops you off at the first mall outside the industrial zone. Most of your colleagues disembark. They intend to buy supplies and nourishment at the RT-Mart, or like you and your "bae," to watch a film.

An equal number of passengers board – they've been waiting a long time; they're headed to the city's downtown area. But for you, this mall is more than sufficient.

The RT-Mart Mall is densely packed with shops. The crown jewel, a Starbucks, is unobtrusively tucked away in the back, in a conical-shaped building, almost as though it is embarrassed at being part of this commercial complex. But no, there is no need for it to be embarrassed at being here. There are other worthies especially in the rear promenade, like Café Royale, a French/

Italian bistro serving some form of edible pizza and coffee. Needless to say, this is where trendy local adults pose and look "cool" while drinking their lattes.

In front of the mall's main entrance is an open square overflowing with bikes, e-bikes, scooters, motorbikes of every shape and size, some of which are dilapidated beyond recognition.

The square gives way to sprawling dead grass and dirt, a bumpy paved road, an abandoned construction site. On the grass, and along a smaller makeshift pedestrian path, dozens, possibly even a hundred or more, unlicensed vendors mercilessly hawk their wares and snacks. At first sight of the city order patrol, these vendors, no matter how old or infirm, will thrust all their merchandise into a cart or on their own backs in under five seconds. They will scatter either by motorized means or by the strength of their own legs, sprinting as if they were trying to convince the Olympic Committee to consider them for a team spot. If you are so unfortunate as to get in the way of one of these terrified people as they flee, have no doubt you will end up with your head trampled upon.

All in all, the atmosphere here is carnival-like. Above, in the night sky, a remote-control airplane dips, flips and somersaults. It makes a sound like a motorboat in the sky, only the sound is more compact. The man controlling the toy plane sells them for a living.

Opposite the mall a large desolate expanse, an abandoned construction site, and beyond that the elevated high-speed rail, which takes the sleek, ultra-fast trains to Shanghai. Past the track are more dense suburbs. On one of these, a tall high-rise, a red dot of light quivers and swings back and forth, coming to a rest near the fifteenth floor. You look and see that the mysterious point of light originates from the carnival. A man has a cart full of powerful lasers and disco balls. All these people come out every evening to catch the money that falls out of the pockets of the factory workers and other well-to-do people with steady jobs and income. People like you.

"Should we go buy tickets first?" you say, as you follow Q.

"I bought the tickets on my phone already," he replies, with the suaveness of any young man who knows he has just impressed his soon-to-be woman.

You feel silly. Nobody buys tickets at the theatre these days, where the ticket prices are always double what you pay with the apps on your phone. Q is savvy. He's happy to show you the tickets on his phone. Sure enough, the seat numbers are already assigned to you both. Despite his rather unappealing face, puffy body and incessant smoking, you're beginning to like Q. Evidently his wily tricks are working.

A man selling personalized mugs from a cart catches your attention as you're walking by.

"Little miss! How about a memory mug for you and your handsome guy? I take a photo of you two, and stamp it on this cup, see? No better way to celebrate young love!"

"No," you say, "we're not a couple."

"Yeah," says Q, "let's have a photo, that way we can remember our first time together. It's a good way to memorialize our romantic date, don't you think?"

You don't say anything, because you've never had your photo on a mug before. Just the thought of your photo on a mug seems novel and special. You know it's a waste of money. But why not? After all, you're having a romance, and isn't wasting money what romance is all about? You nod your head in consent.

"Stand closer together," the hawker says. "I'll take a photo now." Q tries to put his arm around you, but you shake him off. In the end the photo looks forced and uncomfortable. The lighting is wrong, the resolution is bad, there are people in the way. But no matter, the hawker is hard at work pressing the photo onto your mug.

Q pays the hawker – it's twenty-five yuan, the price of a movie ticket. Oh well, flush. The sound of money down the squatting toilet.

The mug is all right, but not what you expected. It doesn't look that great, but it's yours, like a son born with a crippled leg.

"It'll look better after a few washes," promises the hawker.

On to the movie theatre. You walk to the main entrance of the RT-Mart Mall. Inside, the KFC is to the left, and on either side a whole slew of restaurants, cosmetics stores, jewellery stores and an escalator going down to more clothing shops and the RT-Mart. The movie theatre is inside the complex, on the third floor.

Upstairs, Q, well trained by the heady forces of capitalism, swipes his phone against an automated movie ticket machine, which immediately dispenses the tickets. Together, you join the crowd that collects like liquid at a stop where the ticket collector stands, barring the way. The ticket collector is like a palace guard, emotionless, immovable, a soldier holding the battle line for all time. Precisely five minutes before the movie begins, not one second earlier, even if you need to use the bathroom inside, the cord is pulled back. The herd is released.

In the dark, you watch the movie with a sort of glee, sucking in every pixel of Daniel Wu–infused light that hits your retina. Behind you a man talks on his phone, but you don't notice so entranced are you by the moving picture. Then, all too soon, before you have had your fill, the ceiling lights come up.

But wait! The movie is not over, you want to shout. At exactly the best scene, the ending, the staff hit the light switch. You blink and lean forward, trying to catch it, the emotional climax. The movie is still playing, there are still ten seconds left, the most dramatic sequence, but the lights have washed out the picture and you can't see it. Staff stand at the side, arms folded, annoyed that you are trying to watch still. Others are leaving, accustomed to this situation, why not you? Finally, saddened by this untimely end of Daniel Wu, you join the crush of people at the exit.

It's only now that you realize you're holding hands with Q. Somewhere in the dark movie theatre, he slipped his hand into yours. This realization scares you. You twist your hand away.

"I really have to get home," you tell him. "It's late."

"Don't you want some octopus balls first?"

No, you don't, but the octopus ball stand is closed, anyway.

It's so late, past ten thirty. Only vagrants and mischief-makers are up so late, which one are you?

The last bus going to your dorm has already departed. No choice but to catch a small three-wheeled motor cart back. Lucky for you, there's a couple of them left, waiting at the main entrance.

The drivers are all stocky, barrel-chested types with brown-red faces. They may have been jovial earlier in the day, but now, in the late evening, they are subdued.

You know the price to get to B Dorm. You hop in and confirm the price with the driver. The driver retorts with a higher price, perhaps because now he sees a male and female pairing. He has the upper hand. The boy won't want to haggle and be embarrassed in front of the girl, or vice versa. Still, you stand your ground. Soon, before your iron will, the driver has no choice but to yield.

The little metal red frame of the cart fits the two of you snugly, though if you were six inches taller your head would bump against the top of the cardboard-like metallic cover. Everything rattles around you as the driver sets out.

# X. HELP WHEN COMRADES
# ARE IN DISTRESS

From that night on, the night of Daniel Wu, you're pleased that you have a boyfriend. This is your life, consumed with work and your new boyfriend, Q, Daniel Wu, "Ryan Reynolds" and "America."

Over the next week you see Q almost every night. He waits for you by the soy milk stand, and you have something to eat together. He always pays for the meals, like every level-headed couple. You let him hold your hand. The skin on his palms is coarse but you have learned to like it.

You are in love. Contrary to popular belief, love is not always shameful. Now, in your eyes, you see everything differently. B Dorm, which before may have been a tiresome place, is now a playground. You no longer notice its hordes of workers and rude motorcycle taxis. No more the stench of urine and fish excrement. No more the never clean boulevard pavement, unsightly stickers, the men peeing under the staircase. You don't notice the metallic tang in the air, caused by the clouds of heavy carcinogenic metals swept up and dispersed over your head like farm planes over crop fields. No, you don't notice the pain in your stomach that has persisted until now, a dull ache that is probably a malignant tumour waiting to kill you. You don't notice that despite working twelve hours a day, twenty-six days a month, you still go hungry every night because you send so much money home to your parents and do not have enough for food. Yes, love can sometimes be useful.

But when one's luck is on the rise, others may not be so fortunate. While you're thinking to yourself that finally you are enjoying life, your friend Bo Bo isn't doing too well. Bo Bo is crying. You don't know Bo Bo's crying, but you will soon enough.

You're sitting in Taiwan Sushi. You're eating something resembling sushi in name and appearance, but which tastes closer to mayonnaise and under-cooked rice pancaked together. But this is the only sushi you've ever had, other than the shop on People's Road, and this tastes just the same to you. It doesn't taste good, but perhaps the satisfaction of eating something "foreign" excites you. If they had an "American" food stand, you would no doubt even elect to suffer that torture, enduring their infamous "fried ketchup" dish every day for breakfast and dinner, and their "corn dog" for lunch.

A message pops up on your phone. Then a second and a third – urgent short bursts of simplified characters. You take one look, sweep your uneaten sushi into your takeout box, wipe your mouth with the napkin that feels like plastic. Your mouth is full still, you mumble something as you leave the stall. The young server wearing the orange apron who fixed the sushi for you pretends not to look as you pass by.

You find Bo Bo in the dormitory room. Fortunately, another of your bunkmates, Apple, is already there comforting Bo Bo. Apple looks glad as you relieve her.

"It's his parents," Bo Bo says. She's sobbing; she chokes the words out. Relationships are so complicated. You hug her, you hold her hand, but it doesn't stop the flood of tears.

"What happened?" you ask.

"His mother, his father, they don't approve of me. They want him to marry someone closer to their hometown. My family is in Hebei. They're in Hunan. It's too far, they said."

A few letters, that makes all the difference. You don't know what to say. She lets out a prolonged sob that gets caught halfway through in her throat. She accidentally expels a gob of liquid, which runs down her nose. You reach to get a thin tissue from her tissue box, which is covered in a cheap fabric cover. The tissues are spent. She wipes her nose on her sleeve.

"No, don't do that. Wait, I have some," you say. On your bunk, you find the roll of toilet paper; it's scratchy, the two-ply separating upon touching it. You break some off along the perforation, which serves no purpose – it tears diagonally.

You sit back down with Bo Bo, holding her hand. You bundle the blanket up around the two of you. The blanket is so cheap, the material itches your skin. It's the same as your own blanket. The covers are made from polyester or some other cheap versatile composite fabric, dyed in bright colours. She has an old comforter, the material is richer, but it's in tatters, the stuffing exposed. It's bad to breathe in directly – the fibres get into your eyes and mouth and lungs.

There isn't much to say, not much to do, other than to rub your hand on Bo Bo's back and squeeze her slim quivering shoulders.

"Can't you move to their city? Tell his parents you'll move there and live in his hometown, isn't that all right? If you really love him, you can, right?"

"It doesn't matter, my parents won't agree to that."

"What does he say?"

"He says our relationship is more than just a relationship of the two of us. He says we have to be responsible and consider our parents. But what I don't understand is I met his parents before, and it was okay. Now it's not. They don't want me to be with him anymore, that's what he says."

"Does he love you still?"

"He says so. But he doesn't think it's practical for us to be together anymore. They don't want to buy an apartment outside their hometown, anyway."

In time Bo Bo's heart-wrenching crying ceases. It's easier for her to calm down with you there, holding her, you who are her big sister. By the time the other bunkmates appear, she's quiet, she's sleeping. You stay holding her. The two of you hardly fit on her small bunk.

"We'll go to Shanghai," you whisper. "I'll buy us airplane tickets to go to 'America.' We'll get away from all of this."

Don't use false promises and bad tactics to comfort friends, dear Little Comrade.

In her sleep, Bo Bo smiles slightly. You wipe your own tears, and think about Q. You'll have to leave him behind when the time comes. You'll have to leave behind your mother, father and younger brother. You think about Bo Bo and if she'll be happy in "America."

# XI. EVERY QINESE CITY HAS MUCH TO ENJOY

When Bo Bo is feeling better, you help her clean her bedsheets. You take the blankets in your dorm room, the ones stained with tears, and bundle them downstairs.

Outside, you go to hang them on clotheslines between two scraggly trees. But wait, others have already done that. So you drape the blankets over the dusty, dying shrubs and bushes. You need to air out the blankets so that mites don't start infesting. In a room of eight young women, who work every day in a factory, things begin to smell. The linen needs to be put in the sun. Even through the dense smog, the sun's rays will still disinfect and kill. Everything needs to be aired out, especially the blankets.

You were planning to spend the day with Q, but Bo Bo is more important.

Down in the courtyard of B Dorm, which is secured by the twenty turnstiles from the food stalls and the boulevard, you and your best bunkmate friend use two old rackets to hit a shuttlecock back and forth. Bo Bo seems to cheer up. Today is Sunday. Many workers have left the dorms to head downtown. In a bit you may do that too, if Bo Bo is willing. The sheets will be aired out by the time you return.

Even if you don't buy anything, it'll be nice to walk around. The bus downtown is the same one you took before, 210B. This time you don't get off at the RT-Mart. You wait until the bus takes you to the old train station in town, where you can transfer buses and take Buses 1, 4, 6, 23, 106 or 108 all the way to People's Road. That's the main thoroughfare, lined with shops and frequented by many city dwellers.

Bo Bo and you get off at a waterway bridge that spans a tiny river, a tributary of the Huangpu Jiang, which leads eventually to Shanghai, and then the Pacific Ocean.

The low river bridges here prevent anything much larger than a rowboat from passing under. Along the lowered embankment a pedestrian path runs. The road is up top, and set back are the shops, on the opposite side of the road.

The pedestrian path following the river under the bridge has intricate wood carvings, a panelled history of Qina, your country. But nobody goes down to look at it because it reeks of urine.

You and Bo Bo walk along People's Road, elbows clasped. You don't feel too old to be holding hands with your best friend in public. Bo Bo is trying to have fun, but she's already tired. She wants to sit down and have a rest.

In front of a store, she removes the surgical mask that she has been wearing the entire time you have been outside. She wears it because it's what all pretty girls wear. The mask acts like a veil, it ignites people's imaginations. All they see are the cat eyes – the mystery grows. Besides, it makes her feel safe, like a security blanket, covering her so that others cannot see. Also, why should she let all these passersby, people she doesn't know, get a free glimpse of her beautiful looks, while she receives nothing in return?

In one of the four KFCs within a ten-minute walk, you sit by the rear window. It's like any KFC anywhere in the world, but you don't know it. Only this KFC also serves purple taro pie. It serves egg tarts with their curvy, perfectly toasted pastry ridges and delicate yellow filling. Everything is familiar and comforting.

Bo Bo holds her head in her hands. "I've decided I'm going to quit my job at the factory," she says. "I'm never going to talk to my ex again. I'm going to make lots of money on my own and show up my family. I'll show him up too."

She shows you screenshots of WeChat messages she sent to her ex-boyfriend. The messages declare that their relationship is over. She's given up on him, she doesn't want to be with him either. Most damning of all, she shows you that the unrepentant young man has been blacklisted from her WeChat account, the electronic social media equivalent of banishment to eternal hell. Not only that, she is upset at her parents as well for various emotionally convoluted reasons. She tells you she plans to move out of the factory dorm and live in the city on her own.

You're her big sister, you've got to give her some advice. What will you say? Bo Bo has expressed interest in becoming a bum; a social outcast; a lone, solitary woman of child-bearing age with no roots, no husband. You should be alarmed, but you are not. Why doesn't she want to go back home, marry, have children? Devoid of family ties, of a caring workplace, she will surely turn to ruin. The irrationality of the female mind, in the ultimate analysis, is inexplicable. You have no words to offer her. As is said in "America," this is a case of the "visually impaired leading the visually impaired."

At this moment, curiously enough, a foreigner enters the premises. It's a handsome guy, blond hair, green eyes. You notice him even before he is through the glass door. He's wearing a tan suede jacket, hiking boots; he's got a dashing smile on his face. Nobody pays him attention, but everyone adjusts their posture imperceptibly. Everyone strains not to look, except you.

You are staring, slack-jawed, at the white-faced man. You are awestruck, wondering if he's from "America," and if he is, where he lives in "America," and what he does, and if he knows "Ryan Reynolds," and perhaps if he isn't even a relative of the princeling himself.

But soon your interest wanes. He has disappeared into a nook of the shop, where your prying eyes cannot invade his privacy. Disappointed, you turn back to your own table and try on Bo Bo's mask out of boredom. You look at yourself in the video display of your phone. The folds of the soft cotton mask obscure your mouth and nose. Only your eyes and forehead, with its bangs of black hair, are visible. You pose and take a few photos. Bo Bo talks while eating the KFC food that she doesn't like, that she wishes she hadn't ordered. She's indulging herself. She doesn't have money to spend on KFC, but she was hoping it would make her feel better about the breakup, but it doesn't. It makes her stomach feel greasy and bloated. She looks uncomfortable. She doesn't look so pretty.

In the middle of the floor, other patrons line up, preparing to vocalize their orders when it is their turn. The counter staff and cash registers are always busy. Where do all these customers come from? How do they get money to eat this expensive Western food every day? It puzzles you. Yet you will never ask; you will never figure it out.

You go to the bathroom. The two sinks, one lower than the other, are outside the bathroom. Inside, you crouch over the squatting toilet. The ceramic plating is slippery with urine, but it doesn't bother you. These toilets are quite possibly cleaner than most other toilets in the city, cleaner at least than those in the factory, which exude an odour that stretches down the halls and bursts out the windows and doors.

Even in the KFC, the odour of cigarette smoke wafts out of the men's bathroom. You have to hold your breath as you pass by. Even though you're used to Q smoking, you still dislike the smell.

In front of the sink, you don't really want to wash your hands. But there are people around. They can see who comes out of the bathroom, who washes their hands and who doesn't. You're not a man, you don't have the privilege of zipping your fly, flicking some water on your hair and fixing it, before sitting down to eat again. You're a young woman, and you want to be cultured. Besides, if you really want to be "American," you'll have to get used to washing your hands. So, gingerly, you turn on the faucet and test the water. It feels cold. You turn it off again.

As you turn around you bump into the handsome foreigner. He grins at you and says in a booming, confident voice, "Buhaoyisi!" You giggle, surprised that he can speak your mother tongue. You blush and hurry back to your seat, where Bo Bo is looking at herself in her phone, flipping through photos of herself in various poses with various filters and decorations, like cat ears, frilly frames, pink borders.

"That foreign dude knows how to speak Qinese," you say.

Bo Bo looks up from her phone and past your shoulder. You twist in your seat to get another look. The handsome foreign guy is rubbing his finger over his teeth.

"He's cute," Bo Bo says. What she means to say is that he's gorgeous. His eyes, his clear skin, the expressiveness of his features, it makes both you and your best friend tingle and your hearts ache. "You should ask him for his WeChat."

"You think he has WeChat?" you say.

"I bet he does," says Bo Bo, "if he can speak Qinese. Anyway, how do you know he can speak Qinese? Did he ask you out for dinner?"

"Lower your voice, he might hear you."

"So he did ask you out to dinner?"

"No, of course not, I don't even know him," you say. You're annoyed by your friend, but excited at the same time. "Anyway, I've got Q. You're the one that needs a boyfriend. You go talk to him."

"Get real, I don't want to talk to him. I don't like foreign men. Too hairy. And they smell."

Now you're laughing and Bo Bo is laughing. "Quick, let's take a selfie with him in the background, while he's not looking."

The two of you huddle together and, surreptitiously, you succeed in taking the shot with the white-faced man unaware.

When the foreign man walks by a few minutes later, he looks at you as he passes. He's smiling at you, you can feel it, but you don't look up. You're chatting with Bo Bo about something else. You've both forgotten about the foreign man with the hairy chest.

Outside you take Bo Bo by the arm and walk around, eventually coming to a park. You stand there, annoyed by the park's largesse of space, its wanton disregard for the shops and fashion boutiques that might have been.

Even though you are young and don't use the park, you can still appreciate it. Look around. You see the city's elderly folk. How nice it must be for them to have a place to relax under the sun together and enjoy their last years. Soon, when the sun starts to set, the mothers, the sisters, the aunts, the grandmothers and the male counterparts will begin to dance, to do their synchronized act, a mishmash of what might be known in "America" as line dancing, flamenco, ballroom and even calisthenics. Presently, the elderly you see pace in circles, keeping their bodies in shape. From six in the morning, they come and go. Notice that old, grey-haired man. He has on a white glove, a cloth glove dirtied from use. He pats the tree in a rhythmic motion. Pat pat pat. What is he doing? You cannot answer, it is a mystery to you. Beside him, three men practice kung fu in slow motion. One wields a sword. How noble!

But why does all of this bother you? Is it perhaps because you fear a day when you too, old and grey, may be here? A day when you are well past your prime, when you are married and have children of your own. Imagine yourself in the dance formation, with a chunky waist, with formless clothes, trying to do a half-spin. Ask yourself, do these people, your elders, look happy? Will you be so happy when you are old? How can anybody find such contentment? Yes, others do not have to fly around the world to "America" to be happy. Maybe they are happy because they have had a fulfilling family life. Maybe that is what you should strive for, when you answer your mother's phone call next time.

Also in the park are some parents. They sit and stand under the shade of the trees. They aren't blocking the path and they aren't harassing you.

They seem to be protesting some injustice. Look closely at the sheets of paper in their hands. Are they joined in solidarity against a common enemy of the nation? The evil Japanese? The uncouth Americans? No! These parents are working tirelessly on behalf of their daughters. Have their daughters gone missing? Have they been kidnapped by religious warlords? Have their daughters been falsely imprisoned due to political persecution? No! Armed with flyers detailing the physical, emotional and intellectual attributes of their daughters, these parents are ever fearful their daughters will become, perhaps like you, an over-the-hill shrew, societal "leftovers." Some spare no expense, printing beautiful colour poster boards in an effort to maximize their daughters' potential allure.

A young, well-dressed man walks by. The parents cluster around him. What's his salary? How many apartments does he own? Where's his hometown? What make is his car? These are the crucial questions to be answered. True, our country has an imbalanced gender ratio favouring the female, but there is always a dearth of eligible bachelors, men with a tidy income waiting to be fawned over by new in-laws.

The accosted gentleman inspects the photogenic daughters being stuffed in front of his face. He wants to take a good look, to get an idea of what is on the market. All that is required is the exchange of a WeChat contact, or a phone number. The subsequent meeting will take place at a date and place yet to be determined. Just like the market economy, your fellow citizens are efficient and down to business when it comes to love.

Reflecting on these lessons, you and Bo Bo head back to your dorm. When you get home you find your blankets have fallen off the shrub. You think it was the wind that blew them over.

# XII. VISIT RELATIVES WHENEVER POSSIBLE

Spending time with friends is all well and good, but you should never neglect to do the same with family relations. Besides, it's been months since you last saw your parents. Didn't you promise your mother that you would visit her at the next opportunity?

Duanwu Festival has come, and it's a chance for you to fulfill your mother's wish. Fortunately, travelling to see your parents is easy. A short train ride brings you into Shanghai and from there you take a bus to Chongming Island.

On the bus, out the window, you see hardly any traffic. The island you are going to is not a busy place. It's so remote from the city that it doesn't feel like part of Shanghai.

The bus speeds across a seemingly endless bridge. All that can be seen is an impenetrable grey fog. You look out the window, off the bridge, but you cannot see water. You wait for the air to clear, but it never does.

When you do see water, it does not look like water but like a field that is neither moving nor still. The liquid is an unnatural, rather unfortunate colour, if it can be called a colour at all. Have you entered a new dimension? No, it is just Shanghai, it is just the Huangpu Jiang.

When you gain enough courage to look again, you see that the road is over solid ground now. No, you are not yet on the other side of the river. You are merely traversing intermediary islands, other strange, desolated wastelands on route to where you want to be.

The sun is getting low. The residences and shanties of people who must live on this land cannot be seen. It is a mysterious place. You see only rooftops, which appear like visions through mist, so low to the ground. The road must be elevated.

Along one featureless stretch, you hear the crackle of fireworks. You look up and see muted, muzzled flashes of coloured light. The smoke of these explosions is indistinguishable from the surrounding fog. Someone is getting married, perhaps.

The mist begins to fade away. You see trees. Now you know that this is Chongming Island. The trees, planted through good city maintenance, help prevent the island from breaking up and vanishing into the surrounding water.

Finally, after two and a half hours on the road, the bus pulls into a more developed quarter of Chongming Island. You see the ferry terminal and a business-style hotel. The streets are wide and well paved. There are more bus shelters and streetlights and intersections. You breathe a sigh of relief. It is all beginning to look a little like the Shanghai everyone knows and loves.

Lucky for you, the local buses are still running and you quickly transfer. The local bus carries you back through trees and fields to an underdeveloped but well-occupied side street off the main road. Across from a dusty post office you find your parents sitting by the curb outside their snack shop, finishing their dinner.

"Eh? You came," your mother says. She does not embrace you in any way, but her affection is obvious. "You finally got your senses back. Good timing, you can help wash the dishes."

Now that you are standing in front of them, they do not bicker with you as they did on the phone. But their displeasure with you still lingers in the air.

Your father, not desiring to say much to you, has some business to transact and leaves just as soon as you arrive.

Your mother is on her feet. She steps heavily into the tiny shop. Her knees are bad, the result of fluid buildup in her joints. She has tried many excellent herbal and traditional remedies, but none seem to have much positive effect.

Go on, Little Comrade, and help your mother. Rinse the dishes and bring them inside. As you do so, look around. What do you see?

Nothing has changed from the last time you were here. Your parents' snack shop has no front wall, and no window. It has a retractable garage-like door, which comes down from the ceiling. The width of the old shop is two strides across and two strides deep, filled with open pantries of every conceivable delicious fast-selling snack like peanuts and dried yam chips, mostly all natural foods.

At the back of the shop is a closet space, separated by a small entryway with a curtain. The closet space has just enough room for a sink and a single gas stove and wok. A ladder goes up into a crawl space above, where your mother and father sleep in separate cots. This is where you will sleep tonight, too.

It may be noted that this island of Chongming is included in the demarcation of Shanghai. Unfortunately, neither you nor your parents are Shanghainese, nor can you be considered Shanghai residents, in fact.

Strictly speaking, your parents are part of the migrant worker population. To be sure, they run a successful business and are well off by any standard. But even though your father's sister, Third Aunt, lives just down the road from here, and even though you and your parents know everyone on the block, and even though your family's history here is approaching two decades, this place isn't your family's "hometown."

Not being registered residents of Shanghai, your parents cannot claim the benefits of real Shanghainese, most important of all the right to send their children to Shanghai's many excellent schools.

Just like other migrant workers unable to buy an apartment in the big city, your parents had to leave you and your younger brother back in their hometown village six hours away so that you could have access to a school that would take you. This is a simple rule of the hometown registration policy that is in effect across the country, which everyone is familiar with.

In your own conjecture, this childhood separation from your parents is why you feel such emptiness, a constant need for affection that can never be satisfied.

# XIII. MAKE NEW ACQUAINTANCES

Now that your parents are in close proximity, you must feel calmer, happier, a whole person as it were. All your worries fade away, replaced by a warm, lovely emotion that washes over your heart. Do you feel it?

Perhaps you do not. Disappointingly, what you feel is somewhat more oppressive, a feeling akin to being slowly strangled.

Still, do not think that child-parent relations in "America" are any better. In fact, with all the independence and freethinking that plagues the people there, ample evidence indicates their family relations are ever on the brink of disaster. This is easily confirmed by studying the characters on any of their popular television shows, the names of which are irrelevant.

In any case, dear Little Comrade, do not be upset with your mother and father for wanting you to get married. Try to look at it from their point of view. A mother and father have only two responsibilities if they have a daughter and a son. The first is to see to it that their daughter is married off. The second is that a bride is found for their son. So what you mistake for impatience is merely a desire to complete their life's work before they die.

If you feel the need to confide in your mother about your boyfriend, Q, please restrain yourself. Only when a man has proposed marriage should you inform your parents about his existence. Then you may arrange a formal meeting where he will have the opportunity to come bearing gifts, proving he is not just some "tire-kicker." Just imagine if he ended up dumping you instead of marrying you, and as an added slap your parents received nothing. Such an outcome would cause your family unbearable shame and make you a social leper.

The next day, you wake bright and early. First, as always, you check your phone. Bo Bo has replied to your message, saying that she has quit her job at the factory. She's moved into the city, just like she said she would. But, being so far away, it means little to you. You cannot process this information. The only other message is from your bunkmate Apple.

Can I borrow your washing tub? Mine broke : (

You come down from the crawl space above the shop and cross the street to use the public bathroom. Your father, having gotten up earlier, pulls up along the street in a small, dilapidated truck, carrying some eggs in crates, boxes of alcohol and a thirty-kilogram bag of rice.

After a short breakfast, you, along with your mother and father, unload the supplies into a tiny storage room claimed by your parents on an adjoining side alley. Here the path is unpaved and dusty, with shanties on both sides, until it reaches and joins with the river.

As soon as the truck has been unloaded, your father goes off again on another errand. You and your mother are left to tend the shop. It's just the two of you, mother and daughter. Your younger brother is in your hometown village, going to a local school there, getting ready to take the college entrance exams. Everyone is rooting for him, as are you.

A little girl comes by and without saying anything, buys some sunflower seeds, which she scoops into a disposable bag. You weigh the bag on an old electronic scale before collecting a couple of coins in exchange. An old woman hobbles by, asks the price of several items and buys four eggs before leaving. The eggs, like the seeds, like everything else that your parents sell, must be weighed on the electronic scale before being sold. It is a regular day. Business is slow, but your parents are able to get by well enough.

Two young kids, one three years of age, the other seven, from a neighbouring shop, sit on the dirty ground at your feet. They each have a plastic container, inside which is a big square slice of a sponge cake. The cake is topped with a kind of whipped cream substitute not made with dairy product, but artificial, chemical, factory-processed materials. They eat the cream substitute only – it tastes the best, the most cake-like of the cake. The rest of the cake is more or less indigestible. Fortunately, this food item was not purchased from your parents' shop, but from another one down the street.

A local neighbourhood dog trots across your field of view. It turns, perhaps keyed by the scent of food, and comes closer. Alarmed, you take a step forward and throw your hands up over your head, stomping one foot threateningly. It's a small dog, the size of a cat, but you're afraid of dogs and this is what you always do when a dog comes near you, in order to scare it away.

"Eh, you're back," says a woman's voice. "How long are you here for? There's someone you can meet."

It's Third Aunt, who your mother has phoned to come over. She has on a padded vest, a villager's outfit, with a worn flowery print. She looks like your mother, except a bit thinner.

Third Aunt wants to introduce you to a certain young man, the son of her neighbours the Wangs. It'll only take a moment of your time, dear Little Comrade. Besides, isn't this why you came in the first place? Let your elders indulge in their fun, even if you won't let them have their way.

At first there was to be a luncheon at a nearby restaurant to mark the occasion, but this plan was scrapped since it seemed a waste of money. Wait until the matter has been settled, then you can all enjoy a meal together in deserved relief.

Soon you find yourself sitting in Third Aunt's little apartment. Across the table is Third Aunt's neighbours' son, Dong, whose mother stands behind him.

Take a look. What do you think? Can you imagine yourself spending every day of the rest of your life with this man? Dong has a smooth, chubby brown face. Although he looks like an overgrown boy, there is nothing much to complain about.

In your vivid imagination, you previously thought he might have some deformity. Perhaps you had conjured up a hideous monster. But, with the plain-looking fellow in front of you, there's no denying it. You have run out of excuses.

Only, for some inexplicable reason, you don't seem to feel any attraction. Not to put too fine a point on it, but there's no "chemistry" between the two of you.

Dong doesn't like you very much either, it appears. He doesn't exhibit the kind of interest and physical attraction that emanates from Q. This much you can tell.

"Did you have lunch yet?" says the young bachelor.

"Yeah," you say.

"What video games do you play?"

"I dunno."

The conversation flounders around these opening remarks. Soon the awkward meeting is brought to a close.

Afterward, your mother is pleased. You don't say anything to her, nor do you provide definitive answers to her probing questions. She is considering dates for a wedding, asking your opinion about wedding gowns and the like. You listen without protest, but also without giving your consent.

"What do you think? Do you like him?" she asks.

"I don't know."

"What do you mean you don't know? What's not to like? He's perfect for you." She throws her hands up. The shame you bring to your family is endless. Have some sympathy for your parents. Imagine the kind of pressure they must get from neighbours and relatives. Every occasion, celebration or holiday; every accidental meeting in the street brings about the same unanswerable questions.

"Has Little Comrade gotten married yet? My daughter got married already. We got three hundred thousand yuan as the bride price. How much will you ask for?" Or "How many children does she have? My daughter has had two boys already. What's wrong with Little Comrade? Do you need some help? I know a good doctor. Is she still working at the factory? What's her salary?"

These questions, asked daily by neighbours, serve to poke and prod your parents, allowing each neighbour to weigh and compare their own situation with that of your family. With each question your family loses face and the neighbours gain standing. Of course, you are aware of this "face" idea, right, Little Comrade? That is, making others jealous of your own fortune. This is a long-standing societal goal, essentially the reason society has functioned harmoniously and productively for thousands of years. Please remember that.

In any case, with this dreaded event out of the way, your time on Chongming Island passes rapidly. Soon, as unceremoniously as you arrived, you depart.

Your father says he will drive you to the ferry terminal on the back of his motorcycle. The bike is not unlike those big hefty motorcycles that wait around at the entrance of the factory dormitory.

As you depart, the other shopkeepers call out in a friendly manner. Everyone knows you here. They all express regret that you are leaving so soon. But there is nothing to do about it. You've got to get back to work at the factory.

The wind rushes against your face. Even though you and your father have your differences, you trust him. You remember childhood rides, especially in the summer months, when he would take you and your younger brother, the two of you squeezed on the back, on rides to feel the cool wind after dinner. Along these country roads you recall weaving in and out of traffic. You never felt like you were in danger. You didn't have to worry about anything back then. Now you are older, you have to confront your adulthood, get married, find someone else to fend for you. You cannot get a free ride from your parents your whole life, dear Little Comrade.

Your father drops you off at the ferry terminal. You are left alone with the crowds to buy a ticket. Many people want to go to Shanghai. The ferry is faster than the long-distance bus, which you rode on the way over. If there is no space on the ferry, you will take the bus.

Fortunately, you succeed in buying a ferry ticket. Ticket in hand, you push your way up to the front of the line. If you don't rush to the front, someone will take your seat. It happens every time. Even though this ticket guarantees the ticket holder a seat, there's always a fight.

You hike up the metal stairs to the upper deck. Below, on the lower deck, automobiles are parked. The ferry will take these vehicles from Chongming Island to the Shanghai port.

Once they have parked their cars on the ferry, the drivers of these cars will race to the upper deck where the ferry's seats are. They don't have a designated seat, these drivers, but they will take a seat anyway, if they can.

You don't want one of these annoying people to take your seat. An old lady is in your way. You have no choice but to gently squeeze by her. You can feel her resisting. Just use a little more force, dear Little Comrade. Don't hurt her, but let her know you mean business.

Your seat is in the middle row and luckily no one has taken it. To the right of you, a few rows back, an argument has already broken out.

Half a dozen people are in a yelling match, neither side giving way. Both groups say they have tickets for the seats. What is the confusion? They have different times on the tickets. They cannot resolve the dispute.

The boat is underway. The only crew members present are manning the concession stand. For sale are wieners, popcorn, drinks and instant cup noodles. All the other boat crew are mysteriously in hiding, perhaps to avoid dealing with the angry passengers.

A dozen people stand around cluttering the aisle next to you. At any moment the tense yelling may devolve into a scuffle, with angry men and women grabbing fistfuls of hair and shirt collars. Keep your hands near your head, dear Little Comrade. If someone comes crashing your way, you will be in a better position to protect yourself from any flying debris.

Somewhere past the halfway point, the argument loses steam. The losers, the people standing around, realize the ride will be over soon. There is no point making a fuss any longer. You don't know where they go, but they have disappeared to some other part of the boat.

The ferry crosses sluggishly over the water. As it approaches Shanghai, the ferry terminal emerges from the smog like an unreal vision. All you see are smokestacks with billowing clouds spouting forth. Beside these are enormous industrial cranes. There is nothing else, none of the city is visible at all.

# XIV. A USELESS FRIEND
# IS NO FRIEND

The rest of the journey, from the ferry terminal to the subway to the train station, back to the small city where you work, passes without incident, much to your relief.

Upon arriving back in your dorm, you're a little saddened to realize that Bo Bo is no longer there. She has indeed quit her job, succumbed to whimsical ideas, a victim of her own self-destructive ways.

It only occurs to you now that you, a useless friend, did nothing to stop Bo Bo from leaving. You can only hope that she will realize her mistake sooner or later. Check your phone, has she written to you? No, she hasn't. Send her a message, asking if she is all right. You wait for a reply, but there is none. Perhaps she's in the city, just like she said, already working at a different job. You look sadly at her empty bunk. Tomorrow another worker will take her place, do not worry. The economy will continue despite this minor setback.

Back in your routine at the factory, relieved that you have visited your parents and that you can get on with your life, time passes quickly.

When it feels like one holiday has just come and gone, another one is already here.

It's Qixi Festival, but it's not a real holiday, because you get no time off work. But anyway, it's a day especially celebrated by young couples. In "America" it may be known as Valentine's Day, although the calendar dates of these two holidays do not coincide.

Some of our young couples celebrate Valentine's Day, such as the one they celebrate in "America." But you are impatient. You take whichever one comes first, or maybe both, fortune willing.

You can't help thinking how Bo Bo is alone this year and you are not, lucky you. She will have to be the jealous one this time, wherever she is.

Qixi is based on a romantic story about a cowherd and a weaver girl who are stranded by their unapproving parents on either side of a river. Every year, for just one day, magpies come down and form a bridge over which they may walk and be together. But this beautiful myth is not so interesting to you. You just want roses from Q.

"How many girlfriends have you had before, Q?" you ask.

He is less than pleased with the direction of your conversation. But to you, Qixi is the perfect time to quiz him on these issues. "You always ask that question," he complains. "Why not discuss something else?"

"Because you never give me a straight answer."

"Fine. I only had four before."

"That's different from the last answer you gave me. Last time you had three. What changed? You started dating another woman?"

"No, it's the truth, I only had four."

"Only?" you say. "That's a lot, okay. I don't want someone else's used goods."

"Come on, it's Qixi Festival. Give me a break. Don't you like your gifts?"

"Yeah, but you could have bought more roses." You hold up the one flimsy rose with its transparent plastic wrap and cheap ribbon. You always wanted someone to give you a rose, but now that you have it, it doesn't seem very special to you. You are also wearing a cheap necklace that he bought for you.

"Roses are expensive today, especially expensive," he says. "Ten yuan for one. Usually, it's not even half that price."

"Really? Not even half? Where do you usually buy roses? How come you know how much they usually cost? You know the price of them really well – you must have bought a lot for your girlfriends before. But only one for me, is that all I'm worth to you?"

"It's not that, you're confusing me," he says.

"Don't change the subject. Tell me about your first girlfriend."

Possibly it's seeing Bo Bo go through her breakup. Possibly it's that you've been with Q now for some time. But your previous innocence has vanished. You didn't know anything before about relationships, but now you are a veteran of love.

You have matured. You notice when men look at you, you can feel their desire for you. The self-confidence you lacked before has flooded you with a new sense of power. You dress differently, too, like a woman who has no sense of shame.

"I forget her," he says. "I don't even remember her name."

"Your first? And you don't even remember her name? I don't believe it."

"Actually, I never knew her name, she never told me, we just dated once, we didn't even hold hands. Maybe it's better to call her just a friend."

"Did you kiss?" you ask.

"Yeah, just once."

"Well, that means girlfriend boyfriend then, obviously. Who are you trying to trick? I'm not that dumb."

"Why does it matter? It was a long time ago. It wasn't even here, it was at school, in Nanjing. She's long gone."

"So she was a college student, right? You like college students, so why date me? I'm not even a graduate. I'm uneducated."

"It doesn't matter to me, I like you."

"You like me? Not love me?" you say. He doesn't reply; he looks away. Possibly he's annoyed with you, possibly he doesn't know what to say. Or possibly he doesn't care about you at all, which infuriates you the most. You were joking before, but now you feel genuinely angry. "Do you keep in touch with her on WeChat?"

"Who?"

"Your first! That smart college student you dated and kissed. Don't you keep in touch with her? Let me check your phone to see pictures. I want to see photos of her. I bet she's in your WeChat friend circle."

"I don't have photos, it was so long ago, more than three years ago."

"So you had four girlfriends, and your first was three years ago. That means more than one girlfriend a year. Wow, you really enjoy playing the field then, huh? I can tell by your moves. Four in three years, and I'm the fifth, right? You move fast, you really do. Okay, I won't talk about it, I can see you don't want to talk about it anymore. The only thing is, I never had any boyfriends before. You're my first, so I don't think it's fair."

For Qixi Festival, there's nothing to do, except to have a romantic dinner. You only have the evening together, because it's a workday. By the time you bring the rose up to your dorm room, get changed and come back down to rejoin Q, it's already dinnertime. At B Dorm, Q takes you past the food stalls, out to the roller rink and pool tables, where there are some nicer restaurants.

You are about to have dinner here in the plaza. Out in the square a TV is blaring, people are watching TV during Qixi Festival. Not everyone is so romantic, not everyone has a partner, as is evidenced by the group of dark, red-faced workers who are fixated on the outdoor show. The hawkers are all at work. One or two of them, more shrewd than the others, sell flowers and roses like the one you received out of dirty plastic jugs.

# XV. CELEBRATE FESTIVALS, EAT WELL

The story of the cowherd and weaver girl should be a romantic one, meeting only once a year, walking on a bridge of magpies to be with each other. It seems romantic, but it's not that romantic to you. You think those birds could be hurt; you worry that it's inhumane. What an absurd thought you have, dear Little Comrade.

Before dinner is served, you take time to clean the cutlery, using the pot of hot water. The food comes, it tastes good. The restaurant has some style. Even though none of the restaurants beside B Dorm are upscale, this one has some Sichuan Qinese tables, a cultural minority feel that makes it unique. The tables are all made of wood and the square wood seats have high backs. The meat is imported from far away. The items on the menu are reasonable, but Q is paying, so you don't need to worry about that.

As you eat, you play on your phone, now and then wondering what Bo Bo is doing on her Qixi day. She still hasn't responded to your WeChat messages. She must have a new account. Probably she's too ashamed of herself to speak to you. You think without a doubt she must be a "missy" already, walking the street, looking to lure men into her room for quick money. How sad, you think.

With Bo Bo in mind, you know you need to get what you can out of your relationship before it's over. That's what you have to do otherwise the man leaves you with nothing. Whether it's casual dating or marriage, the rule applies. Make sure he pays upfront for what he wants.

Poor Bo Bo, only twenty-one and already a bag of used goods nobody wants. She got a bad deal with her ex-boyfriend. She should have known better.

You'll have to make sure that doesn't happen to you. You don't want to be humiliated like her. You don't want to be a disgrace to your parents. You don't want to be disowned.

In the restaurant not every table is occupied. But the table adjacent to yours is. Your boyfriend is smoking and inside the restaurant it's stuffy; your lungs and throat sting when you breathe. The men, finishing their meal next to you, light up cigarettes and blow the smoke in your direction. You cough; the smoke burns your eyes.

You want to tell Q to stop smoking. You cough suggestively, but he pays no mind. Finally, you tell him to put out his cigarette.

He looks at his cigarette nonchalantly, then takes a puff. "It's done anyway," he says. He puts it out as if he was going to do that all along. He is annoyed with you. You will not make a good wife after all, he thinks to himself.

More food comes, along with two big bottles of beer. There's a sautéed beef meat sauce, roast chicken dumplings, a shredded pork lettuce wrap – it's all the best dishes that you like. At least you're getting a delicious meal on Qixi Festival.

"You know," you say, looking up from your phone, "now that we're getting serious, I just want to be straightforward, so there's no misunderstandings."

"What kind of misunderstandings?" he says.

"You know, about why we're dating, what all of it means. We all have our responsibilities, to ourselves and our families. You're old enough to smoke, you're old enough to be on your own and working, you're a man, aren't you? So, what are a man's responsibilities?"

"I guess that means working and providing."

"Providing for who, yourself?" you say. You're a bit angry at Q's dense brain. "Look, I don't want to date just anybody. I can't betray my parents like that. I have to know that you're serious about this, that you can buy a house when it comes time to do that, and my parents expect a decent payout, a gift you know. That's how it is where I'm from. It's not just for them, that's what's expected, that's what I want for them too. They raised me, I owe it to them. You know how much money they spent on me all these years? You can't expect them to give me up for nothing. It's not about the money, it's just the right thing to do."

"I get it. I know all about that. But how much is the gift?"

"Well, I can't spell it out for you, that's for you to decide, isn't it? But my cousin Lily, she got married last year and her husband gave a gift of sixty thousand. Her husband's just a small-town man, he's not rich. His parents pooled together their money to do that. And he's lucky because they have a house already. But we're not there, we're here, in the city, and it's expensive here. I want to live here, and can you tell me, if you make only four thousand yuan per month, how you will buy a house? The property prices here are very expensive. At least put the down payment on it, if we get married. My parents won't agree to our marriage otherwise. They're just looking out for me, you know."

"Yeah, we can talk about all of that. It's a good thing, I know," he says. He looks away, and it annoys you.

"I'm only asking you, I'm only talking about this because I care about you, otherwise, if I wasn't serious, I wouldn't discuss it with you. If a man's serious, he's got to raise these things himself, why wait for me to do it?"

"I'm in line for a promotion. It's not too bad, working in the factory."

"Not too bad? You're in B Dorm, that's where all the lackeys work, including you and me. What kind of future can you have living in B Dorm? You have to get to a better position and department, something in management. Do you have any contacts? I know you don't want to talk about this, but how do I know you're serious about me? You've already had four girlfriends, who's to say you won't have another four after me?" Good, Little Comrade, you are beginning to sound like a responsible young woman who cares about her future.

The dinner progresses roughly in this fashion. Q's answers do not satisfy you, so you turn to the bottle of Tsingtao beer sitting on the table in front of you. Perhaps you will find more comfort, more satisfaction with this tart, frothy substance than what Q can provide.

It's Qixi festival, and Q has booked a room in La Viva, the hotel where Bo Bo stayed with her ex-boyfriend on her birthday. It's one of only three hotels in the plaza near B Dorm, if the other two can be called hotels.

"I don't know if we should spend the night together," you say, nervously.

All the confidence you had before drains away at the mention of staying at the hotel. You feel like a lost little girl. You're not sure what he means by this, and why a hotel, what it's for. All you've done with Q is let him kiss you, and already that's enough. You're not interested in anything more with him.

"It's just for one night. Anyway, it'll be fun, it's Qixi Festival. Everyone does it. We both have to work tomorrow morning, so we'll just go there and go to sleep quickly. It'll be more comfortable than the dorm. Besides, I already paid for it."

"Oh?" you say. "That's kind of a waste if we don't go then. But can't you get a refund?"

Q shakes his head. You're a little embarrassed. You don't know anything about that bad word no one ever says: *sex*. Truthfully, it's better that you do not know anything about it. It's a bad subject, and improper to talk about.

Why else would your parents, teachers, aunts and uncles avoid discussing it with you? Why else, in movies, books, TV shows, would they skip those parts?

You've tried avoiding it for so long, hoping you would never come to face it. Even now, as you sit across the table from Q, you're not sure if this "staying in the hotel" idea has anything to do with sex. You're not sure if you're just being paranoid and making it all up. Poor Little Comrade, so many indecent thoughts abound, you cannot control them.

Now you must make a choice.

It is your choice, after all, isn't it? Q is waiting for you to decide. Your head feels light. You shouldn't have drunk so much beer. The waiter comes over with the bill. Q lights up a cigarette and sticks his hand in his pocket like a man, he pulls out his wallet and pays for the meal in cash. He's waiting for you to take his hand, to walk over to the hotel, which isn't more than five minutes away.

"Let's have a stroll first," you say, thinking this will be a good way to clear your head. Q nods his approval and soon both of you are outside. More than a dozen pool tables are arranged in an orderly fashion in the parking lot where you walk. There are no cars to be seen, perhaps because nobody who owns a car would ever visit this plaza, only the factory workers who live next door.

You watch the cool guys smoking, spreading their legs wide to take the shot on the black eight ball. Q asks if you want to play pool. You shake your head – you don't know how to play. He asks if you want to learn. You shake your head some more. You don't like sports. You don't like any sports except playing badminton with Bo Bo downstairs on the grass, and only then for no longer than ten minutes at a time. Pool to you is a sport. Anything physical is a sport and therefore detestable.

This "sex," it may as well be said, is also something physical, and though you've never done it, you're sure not to like it. It resembles a chore – sweaty, dirty, icky, exhausting, bringing no pleasure, only discomfort and annoyance.

But tonight, it's your choice. No one but you will decide. You tell Q that you haven't made up your mind. You want to watch the roller skaters for a while, first. You're at the place where you bumped into Q. It was here, it seems like a long time ago.

You scan the crowds for Bo Bo, but she's nowhere to be seen. You look for her ex, thinking if you see him, you can slap him on the face on behalf of your friend.

On the oval warehouse-like roof over the rink a string of light bulbs loosely hangs like a decorative trim. Even though you don't like doing sports yourself, the loud music, the excitement of the people all around you is contagious. Your head swims, your heart races.

"Yes, okay," you say, "let's go to the hotel. But first I need to grab some things from my dorm room."

Q is pleased, and soon he is waiting for you at the dorm entrance, while you get your stuff.

# XVI. ASPIRE TO HAVE A FAMILY

When you get to your room on the ninth floor, you find your bunkmate Apple lying in bed. Upon seeing you, she jumps up and claps her hands. "Guess what?" she says. "I'm getting married! My mother arranged it. This is the last Qixi Festival I have to spend alone."

There is always a line of boys who want to get married. Like so many marriages in Qina, one day you're depressed, your life has no meaning, and then, poof, magically you are married and you have a lifetime of expectations, of children to take care of, of laundry to wash and clothes to clean, a man to care for.

Will you attend Apple's wedding? Probably not, it's too far away. If you're invited and go, you must remember to bring a red envelope, with more than half a month's wages. Otherwise, it will be too embarrassing.

"I don't think I can go," you say.

"Don't worry, I'll send you photos and write to you. I'll tell you all about it! I'm going to miss you, Little Comrade!"

Probably Apple's wedding will be held outdoors, in front of the husband's father's brick house. They will have red firecrackers lit at the doorway on the dirt, and everyone will take photos on their phones. How exciting, how "down to earth."

Most importantly, she shows you photos of the apartment in the nearby city that the boy and his father have bought. It's a two-bedroom apartment, overlooking the train tracks. It's in an old complex where every door of every apartment is covered with ads and stickers, but it's occupied, every unit is lived in, and their apartment has been renovated inside. There's hot water in the bathroom, there's a vegetable and meat market next door, there's babies and grannies who walk around. Aren't you jealous!

And, too, you will be jealous of the photoshoot. She has already contracted a professional portrait company to do it. They will take Apple and the lucky man to the local park. Under the beautiful, grey, smoggy skies, they will take a hundred photos, have them "photoshopped" by tweaking the colors until the faces are so pure, so white and pristine, that you, dear Little Comrade, will drool in envy. Ask yourself, when they have the happiest day of their lives, where will you be?

# XVII. TOO MUCH ROMANCE IS UNPRODUCTIVE

Time flies, you forgot all about Q downstairs. Hurry back down, what if he's upset with you? You find him by the entrance, looking annoyed. But now that you're here, he's happy.

You too are happy, especially when thinking how Bo Bo is probably in the city, without a boyfriend, probably a prostitute. You feel elated. How lucky you are to have your very own boyfriend.

Remember last Qixi Festival? You spent the day alone, and everywhere you went you saw couples holding hands. Now you are the couple others are looking at. You are the one others envy. Good job, Little Comrade!

Make the most of it by clutching onto your man like one of those "ditzy girls" you used to dislike. Drape your arm over him, like he is the only thing keeping you from toppling over. Enjoy yourself while you can.

You don't know if it's the beer, or if you really are having trouble keeping yourself upright. You forget all about your previous qualms, about Q not having enough money, not being able to buy a house and a car. You'll let yourself forget just for tonight.

"Carry my bag, will you?" You hand him your satchel of personal belongings.

He thrusts the strap over his shoulder. He carries the delicate little bag for you like an obedient husband. You think, even though he's not too bright, he'd make a decent husband, a decent father for your children. You don't quite know how children will come to be, but it will be painless. It will be instantaneous, like ordering a takeout dinner on your phone, something you hope to try one day.

As soon as you get to the hotel, a strange feeling comes over you. Perhaps it's the dark, dank, unlit stairwell or the rancid, smelly foyer that bothers you. The place is even darker than your dormitory, where at least the auntie who sits at the bottom of the stair knows you. Here, there is no reassuring figure, just some hotel clerk who looks like a very questionable character.

You see Q paying for the room. You think, you try to remember, didn't he say he had paid for the room already? But now, at any rate, it's paid for, you've seen it with your own eyes. Your previous bickering thoughts don't seem to matter much.

"Come on, this way," says Q.

At the very end of the hall, he opens a door to a cramped room with cold tile floors and dreary threadbare curtains. The small bed is squishy and damp. The bathroom light flickers and flickers until it finally turns on faintly. The toilet is unwashed, stained yellow and brown. Everything, no matter what it may be, looks like it has a fine film of some unsanitary liquid that needs to be wiped off. The TV is the only thing that looks usable.

Turn on the TV, it's Qixi Festival. Some programs show romantic specials, including a CCTV Channel 5 news report on young couples in the big city, cities like Shanghai and Beijing.

Sitting on the bed, knees pulled to your chin, you watch the show fully absorbed. You forget about Q, the young male factory worker sitting next to you. At commercials, you turn your attention to your phone, you check out your friends' WeChat Circles. Always keep up-to-date on what others have posted, that's simple courtesy.

You, as well, post the photos you took during the day. You want others to see that you've had fun, though you make sure not to include any images of Q, or any other male in your photos. That hardly needs to be said, since every female in the country knows this rule. Online every woman is single, the photos look more fun that way. WeChat life is a never-ending bachelorette party with all your friends, and, if you're lucky, the occasional selfie with a smiling foreigner, like that handsome one in the KFC. You pull the screen down and down, back so that you can see that photo you posted earlier. You and Bo Bo, smiling together, the blond, green-eyed foreigner is in the background, just like you wanted. Only, you can't see his face. Too bad. Maybe one day you will be able to take a vacation abroad, take as many photos as you want with those handsome green-eyed giants.

You sigh. You don't know when you'll ever have the chance to go abroad. It's something you can only dream about. Don't worry, Little Comrade, sometimes it's okay to have such dreams. If you go on vacation for a short while and come back, it's okay. But don't think about moving for good, or it will affect your work ethic. Being consumed by impossible dreams can be dangerous.

As you find yourself engrossed in the TV program, you feel a hand on your back, Q is making a move. You hardly notice as he unclasps the button behind your neck, the one that holds the collar of your shirt closed. You're laughing at the Qixi Festival *Running Man* special, a wildly popular live action show starring many famous actors and actresses.

In today's special, they have none other than guest celeb heartthrob Daniel Wu. You jerk up in your seat. Maggie Chen, the Taiwanese singer, is chasing Daniel Wu through the streets of Beijing on a clear blue day. People in the street stare and laugh at them. They bound out of cars, duck in and out of traffic. Daniel Wu tumbles into a grassy ditch, everyone is worried, but he's okay. On his back is a sheet of paper with a number on it, like a marathon runner's number. If the paper gets pulled off by one of the opposing team members, he's dead and off the show. He's on Team B, the blue team. He's almost home, almost in the safe zone. You clinch your fists; you bite your nails. It's *Running Man*, so exciting!

You feel something tugging at your chest, it's been there some time but you haven't noticed because your brassiere is thickly padded to accentuate your A-cup bustline. But the feeling isn't bothersome, you simply push away the object that keeps poking you.

Now, on the show, they're tabulating the number of points each team has won, and it looks like Becky Si, a Singaporean pop star, got caught. She'll be kicked off the team. The tag on her back is missing, she's crying. Boo hoo hoo, those Singaporeans are such crybabies. Hey, you think to yourself, wasn't this shot in Suzhou? You're wondering because you recognize some of the streets.

Earlier, you thought the show was shot in Beijing, but the skies aren't so blue in Beijing. It's got to be Hangzhou, you think. Just as you're trying to place the storefront of a building and the cobblestone walk in front of it that looks so familiar to you, which you're sure you've seen before in person, you feel a wet tongue licking your neck like a dog; it makes you shiver.

"What are you doing, Q? Stop it," you say.

The words seem to have little effect on the young male factory worker. You feel a continued licking and pawing on your chest. His breath stinks of cigarettes and onions and pork.

You turn up the volume of the TV, you want to distract yourself, or maybe the show is just that good. You want to catch every word that Daniel Wu says, because this is his first appearance on *Running Man*.

"Come on, take off your shirt," says a voice. At first, you're confused.

Maybe it's you speaking to the TV. You want Daniel Wu to take his shirt off, perhaps.

But, no, it feels like you didn't say anything.

In fact, it's Q talking to you.

"Stop," you say, when Q repeats himself. "Let me finish the show, then we'll go to sleep."

This seems to satisfy your eager lover. But after you watch for another twenty minutes, the pawing resumes. Your passive resistance increases in proportion to the excitement of Q's hands. Push, tug, squeeze, pinch, twist – no matter what the persistent hands keep squirming their way on your body.

"Let's have sex," Q says. "Try it, it'll be fun. If it hurts, just look at the wall and think of something nice."

Before you can respond, Q sticks his hand up your shirt and pushes you sideways. You fall from your sitting position prone onto the bed. He sticks his tongue across your face and ear. You let out a shriek, and try to shove him off you, but he succeeds in stuffing his hand down your pants, which are loosened and undone.

Poor Little Comrade! Take a deep breath.

In "America," what is happening to you is a criminally classifiable act known as "sexual assault," or more specifically in your case, "forcible digital penetration." Here, in your country, it is known by other names, falling under the general category, in most cases, known as "male-female relations." But, unfortunately, all of this valuable information does not save you from your current predicament.

In the hotel room, you are trapped. Q doesn't stop even though you are crying. Instead, he has taken the opportunity to expose himself. Look away! But, no, it's too late, you've seen it. What you see will not be described here, suffice it to say that you feel sick to your stomach.

However, that is not the worst of your problems. Q is, so to speak, "hitting below the belt," a popular boxing metaphor used in "America" to refer to unfair or foul play. In this case, unfortunately, it can be taken in a literal sense as well.

His finger simply refuses to abate in its exploration of your nether regions. All you feel is shooting pain between your waiflike legs.

In front of your face, in a blur, he feels himself in a rapid motion. His hand moves faster than the eye, like a magician. What is he doing? You don't know, you can't fathom. The knuckles of this hand rap against your forehead.

Is he trying to hit you? No, he is in the act of self-pleasure, "spanking the monkey" as it is bizarrely called in "America." Regardless, no matter where in the world, it is a natural act many men engage in.

It seems it will never end, but in fact he is nearing the moment of release. As you think you are dying, that your insides have come out on to the bed, something happens. What, exactly, you do not know. Q groans and his finger retreats from your body as quickly as it entered. From his loins something is propelled with shotgun-like force onto your face.

His whole body, like a husk, goes limp and falls away as if dead. Gagging, you run to the bathroom. Into the squatting toilet you puke all the roast chicken and beef and lumps of slime that you had for dinner. What a shame, a lost meal, undigested nutrients.

But no matter, you can be forgiven such waste under the circumstances. There is blood dripping down your leg; you are shivering. Hurry and lock the door! What if the monster comes in? Your hands are shaking so hard you can barely make the lock click shut. You're shivering still; your face is streaked with tears. You huddle in the corner and sob. You think for certain he will come in and do it to you again. Hours pass, it seems. Were you dreaming? But the pain you feel is real. The blood on your legs is still there. Slowly you stand up. You are in sound enough mind to turn on the water and wash yourself.

When you come out, Q is sleeping in the bed. It's past midnight and you want to leave. But your dormitory curfew is in effect. You cannot get back into your dorm room. You are tired, exhausted, terrified.

With nowhere to go, you lie down and huddle on the edge of the small bed, your abuser still asleep beside you. You're thinking that you've done something bad, that it's your fault. Q is lying there peacefully. If he was the one who had done something bad, wouldn't he run off? You think hard, but you are confused. You can't figure out what's wrong with the situation.

Perhaps all is well. Possibly there is nothing to be worried about. You don't know. As hard as you try you cannot get your brain to think clearly. Your heart is racing still. Through the whole night, up until dawn, you lie awake in a daze.

The night takes so long to pass. Q snores, but it is not the snoring that bothers you. You hear the sounds of the enthusiastic lovers next door. The walls are very thin, like paper. The creaking, the sounds of females groaning, screaming even, reach your ears easily in the stillness of the night.

Remember, this is La Viva, a hotel of ill repute, used by young workers who have no other place to go to spend private time with each other. You are only now discovering what others knew for a fact.

The couple next door is particularly energetic. As you lie on your side, your eyes wide open in the dark, you begin to hear the slow, low, disgusting moans. Silence, pierced by moans of sin, gasps of evil unladylike pleasure. On and on, for ten minutes, half an hour, for one, two, three hours. The slapping of naked body parts sickens you. You feel the vibrations, the thudding as clearly as if they are in your room. You turn to check, thinking they really are next to you. No one is there, except Q, still asleep.

The moaning reaches a climax. Silence follows. You hear heavy footfalls. Someone is in the shower. Tinkling of water, the man is washing himself possibly. But the footfalls come back, closer, to where the bed is up against the shared wall of your room, right next to your bed. The terrible moaning begins anew. They proceed for a second and third round. You cover your head with the pillow, wondering if you will kill yourself tomorrow.

When morning does come, you leave the room without waking Q. You slip out, head over to your dorm entrance. Hopefully the guards will not be suspicious.

You needn't fear, they will not question you. They take you for one of the dozens, hundreds of other lovers. Fret not, your secret shame is safe. You wonder to yourself, as you pass through the turnstile, if you are in fact just another one of these lovers and you are troubling yourself over nothing.

The turnstiles are well illuminated by large focused fluorescent lights. The facial recognition system scans your face. You can see it in the video display. Your face is sweaty, unwashed, scared, brown and dark; your black hair is uncombed and ragged. Is this who you are? Do you recognize yourself?

You pass through the gate. You say your own name like a mantra to keep calm as you walk quickly to Building 1, first on the left. The dorm buildings are so incredibly large. They are cubic in shape, prison-like, almost windowless for their windows are so small and narrow.

You want to get up to your dorm room early before anyone else wakes. You can't let your sleeping sisters know what happened to you, it'll be an embarrassment beyond anything you can possibly endure.

Fortunately, the electric lights in the hallways remain on at night. You make it into the elevator, down the hall, to your room. Crawl into your bed, pull the blanket over your head. No one will suspect a thing! Soon, just half an hour later, you'll be able to rise with your bunkmates, wash and brush your hair, and go off to work in Area 3, Section 4. Another day's work on the assembly line.

# XVIII. CONFRONT YOUR ENEMIES, DON'T RUN AWAY

Over time, though your body heals and the physical pain subsides, your mind is unable to forget. Traumatized, like Bo Bo, you too find yourself wanting to quit your job at the factory, to distance yourself from these uncomfortable memories.

There's a saying in "America": "When it rains it pours." With Bo Bo gone, you're no longer friendly to your roommates. You reply perfunctorily to questions. Already, in your mind, you have left.

Some time, a week later perhaps, you wake up in the morning. You're on the day shift, which is 8:00 a.m. to 8:00 p.m. You buy yourself a cup of black bean porridge, a pan-fried sausage slice on a flat bread bun smeared with sweet brown sauce and covered with an oily egg. You have to eat, because you're on your feet most of the day, you tell yourself. These are your last days at the factory. You'll find another job soon.

Thousands of workers are returning to the dorm in the morning after their night shift. All the food stalls are open. Steam is rising from the vendors' carts. They are always open in the warmer months, though in the winter after 10:00 a.m. they may close until the evening shift change.

All around you are thousands of young people in green jackets, some wearing their caps, some not.

You keep your head down. You walk quickly through the crowds to Area 3, which is a tightly wound nest of factory assembly rooms and offices. Everything is heavily guarded, and without a pass you cannot enter. Without going through the metal detector you cannot enter.

This section contains lines A.31–S.31. Your position is on Line D.31. Some lines have hundreds of workers simultaneously on shift. Everyone is doing something different. Exactly what you are supposed to do today, you will find out now.

During the daily morning meeting, the team leader stands with you and your coworkers, discussing the performance of team members and allocating tasks. He doesn't know that tomorrow you will tell him you quit.

Before you quit, look around one last time. What do you see? You see fully automated assembly lines, state-of-the-art equipment. Workers are there just to make sure nothing goes wrong, to inspect the parts, to double-check, triple-check.

Today you are checking chips installed on the motherboard. Dell is the client, a brand popular in "America." Indeed, most of the lines in Area 3 are for Dell. Areas 4 and 5 are for Huashuo, or, as it is known in "America," Asus. There are other clients, smaller ones like Hongji, a popular national brand, which you are no doubt familiar with.

The worker before you on the line operates a preprogrammed machine. All he needs to do is watch over it. The machine adds the chip to the motherboard at a precise location. The board is passed along to you. You check it. So simple. Dell users everywhere, including those in "America," thank you, Little Comrade.

On and on the line stretches. You cannot see the end of it – it is straight, it bends, it goes on, until the product is cleaned, wrapped, packaged as a final product for the client.

The warehouse-like hall you are in is fifty, sixty, a hundred metres wide. The ceiling is three or four metres high; it has to be high, because of the air exhaust pipes that suck the smoke from the machines that weld.

During the morning, while you work, you worry that Q may come on an errand. Unfortunately, he is already on his way.

In the Quality Assurance Department, he has a bill of materials in his hand that he needs to fill. This is because Dell, the client, wants a mock-up of a new laptop tested. He has to visit the assembly line where he can put in a request to get it done. The line leaders are busy. They will take his order, but they may not get it done right away. He may have to wait a few hours, or even overnight. They prefer to do their own work first.

So Q leaves his office on the third floor of Area 2, passing by the secure door of Team A95, a secretive laboratory. Behind the fortified door elite workers with security clearances work for Yamasun, better known in "America" as Amazon. They are testing the newest model of a flagship product called Kindle, a silly, useless tablet-like device for viewing e-books, which is no doubt an overpriced bourgeois copycat of our domestically manufactured Readboy.

When Q shows up, you see him. He stands there, making eyes at you. When he sees that you see him, he waves. Somehow this simple gesture frightens you. You neither wave nor smile. You duck your head, you turn away. Though the blood between your legs is gone, you can still feel his presence. Your insides hurt. Almost like a ghost limb, he is still inside you, still violating you.

Your phone has many unanswered WeChat messages. You want to delete his contact from your phone, but you don't. Maybe you're afraid that he'll get angry and cause trouble for you. If you block him, he will know.

So you keep your phone in your pocket, where it cannot scare you. When you turn around, Q is no longer there. He's gone back to Area 2, across the open pavement compound, to the enormous building across the street.

At lunch you resolutely decide to quit your job. You need to get away from Q. But where will you go? Your mother and father will pressure you to go home. They won't understand that you are quitting because you want to have a different life from the one that you have now, and a different one from what they imagine. They won't agree that you are not a rebellious child, that you are not irresponsible.

"Yeah," you say. You try to make your voice clear, confident. "I'll come home, but not yet. I found another job." You haven't but that's what you say. Lies all lead to disaster. You have disappointed your mother; you are a bad child. You will go downtown, into the city, you will try to leave the factory life. Fine. For you, getting a job is no problem, you will take the first thing that comes along.

"What other job?" says your mother. "Don't be so stupid, what kind of job will you do? Why leave the factory and then stay there in the city when everyone is waiting for you to come here? What's the point of that? Where will you live? Why not come home if you're not working in the factory, it doesn't make any sense. What aren't you telling me? Did you do something bad?"

Luckily for you, your mother will not say what she is thinking, that perhaps you, her daughter, are pregnant. She cannot say such a thing, because that would admit the existence of that ugly, unspeakable word, the word that makes every right-minded person shudder: *sex.*

"No, of course not, I can just make more money doing something else."

"What's your other job? What job did you find then?"

"It's not set yet, let me arrange it first, let me get settled down, then I'll tell you all about it, okay?"

"You silly girl, you don't know what you're doing; just come back home.

What a waste of time. Don't expect to us to send you any money when you starve."

"I don't need money – I can make enough on my own. The pay is plenty, I'll be fine."

"Who knows what you're up to there – it's ridiculous. Let me just ask you, why don't you come home? If you're not working in the factory, why not come home?"

And in a circle the conversation goes, from the very beginning. You wrangle with your mother on the phone. She says if you don't hurry, Third Aunt's neighbours' son will find another wife. But no matter how many good reasons she bats at you, you dodge all of them. When she cries and sniffles to make you feel guilty, your heart hurts but your resolve doesn't break. When she has finally given up, she passes the phone to your father, and your father does the same with you, only he is angrier, he is not as pleasant as your mother. You feel drained, your whole body is exhausted. You cry, you begin to reconsider.

After the phone is hung up, after you've gotten off your shift, and you're lying in bed and you've regained an ounce of strength, you know what you will say to your team leader after the next morning's meeting. You are a stubborn idealistic young person; you will not be dissuaded. You should give a week's notice, but in your haste to get away from this place, you cannot wait that long.

Your boss will shrug his shoulders. He will not shake your hand. He will not pat you on the back or thank you for your two years of service. He'll say, "Fine then," and look down at his papers to continue his important work. Nobody will come say goodbye to you as you clear your things out of B Dorm, Building 1, ninth floor, Room 12A, except maybe for Apple. She will say bye half-heartedly. She is too distracted, too excited by her upcoming wedding to care about you. Maybe, if you are lucky, she will walk you to the elevator. The others care even less about you; they will pass by you to the bathroom to wash their faces in wide brightly coloured plastic tubs. They will soak their feet in hot water and put on their paper beauty face masks that they bought on sale from Taobao at 110 yuan for ten, the expensive kind, definitely imported from South Korea. When Apple has the chance, she will check your bunk after you're gone to see if you've left anything worth keeping for herself. But all she will find is an ugly looking mug featuring a scratchy, dark photo of you and Q.

PART
TWO

# XIX. ALONE FOR ONE DAY IS LIKE ALONE FOR A THOUSAND DAYS

So, just like that, you are on your own.

You tell yourself you are not stupid like your mother says. For example, you know how to use DiDi Car. You know how to use 58Wuba to geolocate yourself and find the nearest six dozen empty apartments for rent. Just a swipe of your finger, such ease! How savvy you are. As for Meituan, that's a cinch. With the tip of your finger, you can order food from any of the more than one hundred restaurants and nourishment providers within a thirty-kilometre radius of your current location. If you want to cook, you can even select groceries from RT-Mart and have the friendly Meituan delivery boy in his signature yellow-and-black uniform bring them to your door.

Naturally, to do all these things, you need money in your WeChat account, or your Alipay wallet, or your BOC e-account. You have money, albeit not enough to indulge in these conveniences, not enough to bother learning them well. But you have some superficial knowledge, which will suffice for now. Like they say in "America," "knowing is half the battle."

One step at a time, dear Little Comrade. First, you need a job. There's a restaurant that you've been to before, near the downtown area, where you once ate. Why not try there?

The restaurant is on a pedestrian-heavy road. Many restaurants and shops populate this area, but it is not the most "chic" street in the city. It's not shabby either. Anyway, you're familiar with this street because you liked coming here with Bo Bo to a special shop, Clam Hut, to eat the clams sold in cups. This Clam Hut is the cheapest place to get clams, but they're so spicy and the shop is so cramped and smelly that few people can stand eating there.

The place where you ask for work isn't Clam Hut, which only has two employees, it's down the street, an economy chain restaurant called Su'ke, with a blue-and-white storefront.

However, when you get there, the window has no "help wanted" notice.

Not one to be easily deterred, you think why not ask them anyway? Good, Little Comrade, be proactive and you will find your way back into society soon.

The store manager is a solidly built woman in her forties called Manager Mu. "Why do you want to work here?" she asks when you introduce yourself. "A young girl like you should go home and live with your parents. You're not a local, right? Where are you from? Your accent sounds like Su'bei."

"I'm from Jiangsu. I'm on my own," you say. "I got in a fight with my parents and I want to prove that I can take care of myself. I can do anything, I'm a hard worker. I don't mind working in a restaurant if someone shows me what to do."

"Okay, fill out this form then. But you should know, the pay is only twelve yuan an hour." Evidently you have sufficiently impressed Manager Mu. "Come early tomorrow. I'll give you your uniform then and show you what to do."

"All right, thanks," you say. "By the way, do you know where I can find some cheap apartments nearby? I want to rent a small room."

"Sure," Manager Mu says. She directs you down the street to a residential quarter called South Flower Garden. "Try there, it's really cheap."

Out into the world, so brave you are, dear Little Comrade.

You walk down the road. During the daytime the place looks less lively than the evening. After work, people from the nearby offices, mostly young people in their prime, come to eat. Most of the storefronts are restaurants and various boutiques. Half a dozen KTVs, catering to wealthy businessmen, are interspersed throughout; their storefronts are discreet, sandwiched between restaurants and cellphone shops. On the wide sidewalk scooters and bicycles are parked in neat clusters, organized by the frumpy "street nannies" in brown uniforms. Four bicycle repairmen, forearms greasy, occupy the sidewalk behind the bus shelter. They are perpetually there; always afraid someone will take their busy spot. Along the street, cars are parallel parked, demonstrating that the drivers are indeed competent in motor vehicle operation. Outside a fruit stand, a young mother holds her toddler naked below the waist, her arms locking the legs apart, pointing the object away from herself like a weapon. She bounces the toddler up and down; the toddler evacuates onto the road as you pass by.

At the entrance to South Flower Garden, a security guard sits in a weather-beaten swivel chair. He is smoking and chatting to another guard. They are older comrades, their faces look older, perhaps in their fifties and sixties, but more likely they are in their forties. They seem so well at ease, so perfectly content with their current occupation that there is nothing else they would rather do for the rest of their lives. Such a nice peaceful life, made possible, of course, by the glorious revolution and our visionary leader, Deng Xiaoping.

On one brick wall, a billboard hangs, plastered with flyers advertising rooms, some in typescript, some scribbled by hand.

The guards, perhaps because of your pleasant appearance and the bulky luggage you carry, notice you and speak up.

# XX. HELPFUL COMRADES
# ARE EVERYWHERE

"Little sister," says the one on the chair, "are you looking for a place to rent?" He stands up from his chair and straightens the front of his uniform as he steps over to your side.

"Oh, yes," you say. "I'm looking for a small room. The cheapest, in fact. I'm a factory worker, I don't have much money."

"I see, I know," says the guard. "Why are you here then? Why not live in the factory?"

"I left my job. I'm working around here now."

"Sure, I know. That's a simple situation, with an easy solution. Just go down this road." The guard gestures into the South Flower Garden complex. On the left side are low six-story apartments without elevators. Naturally they are this height, because if they were any higher the developers would have needed to install elevators in order to avoid violating city building ordinance codes. How clever they are!

The driveway has parking spaces; it is wide, like a promenade. It continues through the complex two or three hundred metres until it exits to the road opposite.

"You see," says the friendly guard, "you can rent a room up in one of these buildings. Any of these flyers is good, but you have to pay the middleman a commission. If you're not too choosy, you can see if there's one of these storage closets that's vacant. You know, they're to store things for the apartment owners. But some of them have been converted into single rooms. You'd be on the ground floor, it's noisy, but it's cheap. If they ask more than three hundred a month, don't take it."

"Thanks, uncle," you say. "That's really helpful. Three hundred is a good price, I think I can pay that."

"Oh, I'm sure you can. A pretty girl like you. If not, I'm sure there's a handsome boy who will want to pay it."

Little Comrade, the guard is only teasing you, don't be upset. Inside the compound, you walk back and forth at the base of the buildings where there is a row of converted storage closets with locked metal doors, each with a tiny narrow window slit. The windows are all darkened. The inhabitants, if there are any, are out during the day.

Instead of going back to the entrance gate where you came in, you take out your phone and swipe over to 58Wuba. The useful app lists all the available apartments in your selected vicinity. After calling a few numbers, you find the cheapest listing in South Flower Garden. In a couple of minutes a young woman riding a scooter appears.

The apartment sublet she shows you is on the top floor of one of these buildings. "You can hang your laundry out the window to dry without getting trash all over your clothes like the suckers on the lower floors do. Here, the bathroom and kitchen are shared with other tenants. You can rent this room if you like."

There's a sliding padlocked door made of a wooden frame covered with opaque wax paper. The sliding door almost falls off its rail as it is opened. Inside is a bed against a barred window. In the floor is a hideously large metal pipe sticking out from a pit of broken black concrete. The room is next to the communal bathroom. The water heater, which provides hot water for the bathroom shower, is installed in this little bedroom you are being shown. The big cylindrical metal tank hangs over the bed precariously. If it falls while you sleep at night, you will be seriously, even fatally injured. Other than those minor details, the room is perfect. But, of course, the price is too expensive for you.

"Don't you have anything more economical?" you ask the broker. "How about the storage rooms down on the ground floor? I heard those are three hundred. Can I see one?"

She shakes her head. "If you want this room, call me. You can pay by WeChat."

A moment later, you are back outside and the broker is gone. Thinking you'll ask the guards for some help, you begin walking over to the entrance. But on the way there, the door to one of the storage closets opens. Someone comes out. At first you think it is your friend Bo Bo, but the woman is too grubby looking. Her hair is cut shorter. She looks like she just rolled out of bed.

"Bo Bo?" you say.

It's only been a few months since you last saw your friend, but she's so changed you hardly recognize her. At first, she doesn't hear you; she's squinting in the light. It's the afternoon, but she's just woken up. She has a cup and a toothbrush; she squats down outside by the parking curb, brushing her teeth. She rinses her mouth with the water in the cup and spits the water out onto the pavement.

It's no surprise, in fact, that she's in such a state. All single women who don't marry, who quit their jobs in the factory to live a frivolous life of dissolution, come to this sort of messy state. It's such common knowledge, it hardly bears worth mentioning.

"Hey, Bo Bo," you say. "It's me!" You wave your hand and approach her cautiously.

She finally hears you and looks over. But when she recognizes you, she darts into her room and slams the door shut.

"Hey, come out," you say. You bang on the metal door and kick it, making a huge racket. "Come on, talk to me. Why don't you reply to my WeChat messages anymore? I miss you! You know, I quit the factory too, I'm just like you!"

Eventually, when she cannot stand the noise any longer, she comes out, scared at first. Once she sees you are serious about what you said, that you quit the factory, that you are in just the same position as her, she throws her arms around you.

At length, after you have caught up, she shows you her room, which is smaller than a parking space. At the doorway, almost blocking it on the left, is a small desk. Immediately from the right wall, sticking out halfway into the room, is a toilet bowl of irredeemable quality, with no seat cover. Beyond these two objects is the bed, which is made of a matchwood board on a sturdy metal frame, occupying more than half the total space. On the walls the wallpaper is peeled half off. There's a large ugly pipe that comes from the ground up to the ceiling and another one along the ceiling above the bed. The place is cluttered with some of Bo Bo's cheap personal belongings.

"My room is so small," she says. "I'm so ashamed."

"I want to rent one of these myself, there's nothing to be ashamed of."

"You know, this one was empty when I got here, and the one next door is vacant too. I can give the owner a call. He'll open the door for you and you can move in right away. We can be neighbours, just like in the factory dorm!"

Well done, Little Comrade! Just like that, you have a place to live, and a friend again.

"I got a job as a waitress," you say. "What have you been doing for money?"

She shrugs. "This and that. Let's not talk about it."

She takes out an electric hot bowl, plugs it in and takes it outside, stretching the cord.

"Want something to eat?" she says. "You look like you could eat a little something. I don't have much food. Why don't you go to the shop right there and buy a couple of packages of noodles, we'll cook them and have lunch."

Soon Bo Bo is boiling water that she pours from a jug and cooking the noodles. There's no sink, so she fills up the jug from the public restroom across the street. A simple, if not charming, daily chore, which you will have the pleasure of doing as well.

The owner arrives as you and Bo Bo are squatting outside, eating. He lets you into the adjacent storage space. The room is the same as Bo Bo's, but a small AC unit is fixed above the top of the window. It doesn't work, so the landlord doesn't charge you for it. Soon, your business is settled and you unpack your things. When night falls, you tuck yourself into bed and fall asleep.

# XXI. BE WARY OF FRIENDS WHOSE HABITS CHANGE FOR THE WORSE

Over the next week or so you work at the restaurant and get into a rhythm. The manager is pleased with your efforts, even though you often get bored and your mind naturally wanders to silly things, like how to disobey your parents. At least you are keeping out of trouble and contributing to the economy, instead of chasing after foreign men.

One night you're mopping the tiles outside the door when you see Bo Bo. She's come to find you at work.

"Hey, Bo Bo!" you say. "Over here!"

"Hey," she says, coming up to you. "Are you having fun?"

"Yeah, it's okay. I'll be done in a minute. What's that you're wearing?" She has on a tight black dress, the kind of dress that makes male comrades think questionable, unproductive thoughts. Be careful, or you will be influenced by her shameful new fashion ideas.

Soon you are outside walking with Bo Bo on the street. "Come on, let's go to that snack shop we always liked," she says. "You remember? Clam Hut?"

The smell reaches the two of you before you see it. There's a small open storefront, like a window in the wall, and a recessed entryway. The cook is standing there, practically on the sidewalk, cooking clams and oysters and other seafood.

"Let's get a seat."

There's a free table – Bo Bo goes right in and sits down, hunching over the menu, which is pressed under the glass against the table. She hasn't been seated for more than ten seconds when she yells over to the waiter. Ever since leaving the computer factory, Bo Bo's manners have really changed. She's more manly, less feminine, more bossy. It's bad news.

"Two pounds of clams for us and make it quick! Make it real spicy, dump all your hot peppers on, I don't want it bland like last time, it tasted like crud last time."

"Yeah, you again?" says a waiter, who comes out of the closet-like kitchen in the back. "Okay I know, pretty girl, just relax."

"Gosh darn it, I'm hungry. Hey, you, hurry up, I haven't had a bite to eat today since I woke up," she says to the cook. "Waiter boy," she cranes her head around and yells into the closet-like kitchen. "Get us two cold beers, we're thirsty."

The foul language makes you look at Bo Bo. But then you think it's funny. Maybe you want to try cursing too. Beware, it's contagious.

As you're waiting for the food, she takes a toothpick and picks her teeth, and spits into the little trash can at the side of the table.

"So do you want a job at the restaurant?" you ask Bo Bo. "Maybe I can put in a good word for you."

"No, thanks," she says. "You know, to tell you a secret, I already have a job. A good one, I can make lots of money. I'll show you some time."

"Really?" you say. "What is it?"

"Making money's easy. There's plenty of ways to go about it. I'll tell you later if you want. No good talking about it here, too many eavesdroppers. Hey, cook boy, where's our food?" She starts rapping the table.

"It's right here, hold your horses," says the waiter, who brings over two wide low paper takeout bowls full of clams and two pairs of thin transparent plastic sanitary gloves for eating.

"Is this enough?" Bo Bo says, looking down at the menu. "We can order something more, what about the horsefish? I love those, but they're so expensive." She is greedy, no matter how much she eats, she is never full.

Bo Bo already has her plastic eating gloves on and is wolfing down the clams, spitting the clamshells onto the tabletop. The clams are juicy, and there's sauce in the bowls. She makes a slurping sound as she shucks the clams. She eats as though she is a starving wild animal.

"You can tell by the way I eat that it tastes good, right?" she says. The clams go into her mouth as fast as the shells are ejected from it. She shows satisfaction in other people seeing her eat messily. What a shameless woman.

Don't copy her bad manners, dear Little Comrade. But, alas, you eat in a similar fashion. With the gloves on, the powerful aroma of the clams has seized your senses, and you are eating rapidly, almost mimicking Bo Bo's every move.

"Wow," you exclaim, "these are really tasty, I haven't had them for such a long time."

"We can come here more, now that you're living right here. See, aren't we lucky for quitting the factory. Freedom, we can come out every night and party, we can make tons of money and have fun doing it."

Bo Bo hardly has time to take a breath of air. When she has a moment to breathe, instead she drains her beer. She smacks her lips and lets out a satisfied burp. She picks up her empty bottle and looks at it. "I shouldn't drink, I was in the hospital last month and the doctor said my liver is toast, but I always forget." She turns to the waiter. "This is really spicy. Just the way I like it. Make sure you do it like this from now on, I don't want to remind you every time."

Outside, you walk with Bo Bo back toward South Flower Garden. She has on high heels, you notice, and walks a bit slowly. "You sure go to sleep early," Bo Bo says.

"Yeah? It's already nine," you say. Nine is very late, it's when good comrades should be preparing to sleep.

Along the street a couple of young women pass by, dressed in revealing clothing. Bo Bo nods at you significantly as they pass.

"See those girls," she says. "Just like that you know what they do."

"What?" you say.

"Oh, come on. The whole street. Take a look at the KTV over there. Every time you see a pretty missy, ten out of ten times she's working in the KTV. On this street at least. Anyway, it's a good place to make some spending money."

"Really?" you say. "How do you know?"

"I just know, trust me. I've worked there before. That's where I'm going now. I'm working there. Want to come?"

Intrigued, but tired from a full day of working at the fast-food restaurant, you decline.

"No," you say. "I'm tired, maybe next time." You are lucky for now, keeping your innocence intact and unaware of the dangers that await you should you make just one false step. You can only hope that you will continue to be so lucky.

# XXII. FOREIGN QINESE NO BETTER THAN REAL QINESE

Over the next few months, you work afternoons in the restaurant. Occasionally you hang out with Bo Bo in the big new mall across the river.

The mall is a fancy place with swanky shops. All the wealthy locals like to go there. The first floor contains a McDonald's and even a Dairy Queen. Here, Starbucks is front and centre, uninhibited, unembarrassed to be in such esteemed company. Also, many exotic cuisines like Thai food, Greek food and even something called a "vegan buffet," which can only be a kind of perverse invention foisted on the world by a country like "America."

Downstairs is a clean and well-lit overpriced grocery store, containing a wide range of imported food items. There is no need, however, for you to look for "American" pot pie, which you no doubt would enjoy inspecting on a store shelf. Nor is there a need to look for "American" key lime pie, a sort of infamous sugary pie that is so sweet it is almost inedible. Those famed delicacies are, in all honesty, beyond even the reaches of this high-end retailer.

On the upper floors are clothing boutiques and more restaurants. There is even a very big restaurant called New York Seafood Buffet. At two hundred yuan a person, it is well beyond your means. Oh well, anyway, you would have discovered that New York Seafood Buffet has inferior quality food, and the taste cannot compete with Clam Hut.

"Hey," says Bo Bo, as you eat some octopus balls in the food court, which you bought with an e-coupon from Meituan. "I wanted to tell you, at the KTV last night, I saw a foreigner. The same one we saw at KFC, remember?"

"Yeah?" you say as your face lights up.

"Yeah, the one with green eyes and blond hair. I found out his name – it's Steve. He can't speak Qinese that well, heh. All he knows is *buhaoyisi*. I was speaking to him in English. You know, since I left the factory, my English has gotten really good from working in the KTV. I get a lot of chances to practise my English. There are so many foreigners there, mostly Japanese. Anyway, I told Steve about you."

"No, really? What'd you say?"

"Just that you're a cute girl, that you two would make a good couple. I said that you don't mind going abroad with him, you know. That if you two got married, he could take you back home with him. He's from America. We had a big party. Too bad you weren't there. You could have met him. I know where he works, want to go after you get off from the restaurant?"

You're eager to meet this handsome giant in person, maybe he will fall in love with you, who knows? It's a pity he doesn't have a more dignified name, something more respectable like Wang or Dong. But to you, Steve sounds like a magical name, like music to your ears.

You bring an extra change of clothes to Su'ke, and afterwards Bo Bo meets you and off you go.

Waiting at a stoplight, you see a pair of scantily dressed young women. Bo Bo nudges you. "See, they're everywhere," she says.

Bo Bo takes you down a few streets. It's farther than you thought, but you don't mind walking with your friend. "We'll take a DiDi car back, my treat," she says.

You get there. It's a blue storefront, an English centre, with a small glass door with stairs leading up. A young woman sits behind a tall counter with a sleek computer.

"What do you think, should we go in and have a look?" Bo Bo asks you.

You're a little shy, and the people in the office seem so educated, so above you, that you turn away. Don't worry, Little Comrade, you are just as worthy of being there as anyone else.

"Come on, we walked all the way here. I bet that foreigner's probably already off work. You don't need to be nervous. Let's ask at least." She opens the door and you stand behind her.

"Hey, are you still open?" says Bo Bo to the counter girl.

"Yeah, there's one last class. It's the public class, taught by a foreigner. You're lucky. It's free actually, if you want to go up. Just sign your name here. There's still half an hour left. If you like the free public class, you can sign up for lessons. Here's a brochure. What level English are you?"

"I'm advanced," Bo Bo says. "Hey, who's the teacher for this class, a man or a woman? From America?"

"Yeah. Go up and take a look yourself. It's on the third floor, in the Beijing room."

"Heh, America." Bo Bo chuckles. "I guess we hit the jackpot. Hm, so this is where all the foreigners hang out, I should have guessed."

You go up one flight of stairs, which opens onto a landing with four or five small glass cubicle rooms. Each room features the name of a city, like Sydney, London, New York.

Along the staircase, mounted on the wall, are wooden-framed photos of foreign teachers. The faces are all friendly, handsome, beautiful foreign women and men. They look like movie stars, with their strange names written underneath on gold plates. Look away, dear Little Comrade! Their eyes beckon you, calling you to learn English, to go abroad, to travel to that faraway place, "America." Beware, they are like dangerous sirens, do not fall for their trick!

"Hey," you say. "There he is! Steve!" His handsome pale face and blond tousled hair looks out at you. His green eyes are striking and entice you closer and closer. Eager to see him in person, or one of his equally handsome colleagues, you ascend the steps.

"I wonder if Steve is the only foreign teacher they have, now," you say aloud. "I wonder how many are men."

What do you expect, a whole bevy of blond, six-foot-tall, green-eyed, stubbly chinned men? A small private English centre like this in a third-tier town like this, isn't having one foreign teacher enough? And aren't you here to learn English, and what does the gender of your teacher have to do with anything? Maybe you are imagining there is another foreign teacher, a man as handsome as or even more handsome than Steve. Already you can see yourself sandwiched between two giant handsome foreign guys. Get your head out of the gutter.

Up the steps you go, following Bo Bo. On each step of the staircase phrases like "Practice every day will lead to perfection" are stamped underfoot. They exhort you to study hard.

The phrases are written in alternating English and Qinese. At the landing to each floor are posters showing the increased financial success of people with good English skills, and news clippings of stories relevant to English learning, and movie reviews of the latest Hollywood success. On every floor is a water cooler, and some sofa chairs to promote casual conversation and a friendly environment.

Up on the top floor, you can't find the room with the foreigner. About a dozen students are sitting in the Beijing room. It has to be a mistake, because there's no foreign teacher in it, only a local Qinese teacher. There's a glass door at the rear of the classroom. You nudge Bo Bo, who sticks her head in.

"Hey," Bo Bo says loudly to the group of students nearest, "is this the foreign teacher class?"

The students nod. You and Bo Bo enter, sitting at the back, listening. The Qinese teacher at the front speaks in English, but you don't understand any of it. Bo Bo gets fidgety, as do you. The class breaks into groups and begins to do some exercises among themselves.

At the front of the classroom the teacher writes on the whiteboard. At the rear of the room, behind where you are seated, the wall is decorated with mounted movie posters one after another, all in a row. One of the posters has a man with a black sesame face, Morgan Freeman. The movie is *Shawshank Redemption*, an absurd American-made documentary about two worthless criminals.

"You understand any of this?" Bo Bo asks you.

"No, how about you?"

"I don't know. What's going on," Bo Bo says to one of the students, "where's the foreign teacher?"

"Oh, that's him. That's Mark, at the front of the room."

"What, the Qinese teacher? He looks Qinese."

"Yeah," says the student.

Confused and thoroughly dissatisfied with the results of your efforts, both of you wait until the class is dismissed, which, fortunately, happens after only a few more minutes of almost intolerable waiting. Presently, you filter out down the stairwell with the others.

When Bo Bo has a chance, she questions one of the students. "We were looking for the foreign teacher's class, an American," Bo Bo says.

"That's the American teacher, Mark. He's Qinese, though; he looks like a Qinese, doesn't he? I don't really like his class." Some students murmur in agreement, but they don't talk loudly.

"Do you know the American Steve?" says Bo Bo. "He's got blond hair and green eyes, he's real tall. I know he works here."

"Yeah, Steve works here. He went on vacation, though, back to his home city. I think he's supposed to come back next month. Why don't you check back then?" says a female student with a dreamy sigh.

The simple fact that Steve has gone home to "America," even for a short while, crushes you. "But that sucks." Too bad, he's not here, Little Comrade. The love of your short, embarrassing life.

"Excuse me," says a voice. These words are said not in Qinese, but in that international vernacular young people the world over are so commonly predisposed to use, English. You don't understand what has been said, but you see that it is Mark, the English teacher supposedly from "America." He squeezes by in the staircase, smiling at you and Bo Bo. But neither one of you looks at him.

"Oh well, we can come back another time," says Bo Bo. "Don't feel so bad."

Your shoulders slump. Outside, on the street, you wait for the DiDi car. Bo Bo tries to comfort you.

"Nah, that was dumb, I didn't understand anything," you say. "That teacher's English wasn't that good, was it?"

"No. What do you expect? Everyone knows these places all rip the students off; they have phony foreign teachers. Look at this flyer, fourteen thousand yuan for one term, what a bunch of scammers. You'd think they'd be able to hire some real teachers, not fake ones. I bet my English is better than that ugly guy's. What did they say his name was? Mark? Shoot, I need an English name too, then I can teach English."

Soon, having been comfortably shuttled back to South Flower Garden by the DiDi car driver, you find yourself in Bo Bo's storage closet bedroom.

"Come on," she says, "we can have some tea."

You both sit on her hard, uncomfortable bed while she boils some tea in her electric bowl.

While you wait, you look at your phone. Apple, your old bunkmate, has sent you an instant message.

Dear Little Comrade,
Things have been too busy. I put some wedding photos up, did you see them? Such a nice traditional Qinese wedding, I really wish you had been there. Thank you so much for the red pocket money you sent from your WeChat Wallet. I used the money to buy my husband a watch. The apartment is perfect, the furniture is so nice, and we are thinking of getting a new car. I'm so lucky I found the perfect Qinese man. I love him so much. I can't wait for you to visit. I can drive you around. What's more, I have exciting news, I'm going to have a baby boy! Believe it, I'm all grown up now, aren't I?
Talk to you soon!
Best friend, Apple

When you open her WeChat Circle, you see that there are dozens of photos of her wedding. Mesmerized, you flip through photo after photo of Apple and her handsome Qinese groom, and the wedding party. The whole room is red, with red curtains and red costumes. You see a big cake and a traditional tea ceremony. Apple is eating longevity noodles with her new husband. It looks so wonderful your heart begins to ache. That could be you in the photos, but it's not.

Apple must be too busy to answer your WeChat messages. Obviously, she has a life and family, both things you should strive for.

What a pleasant email. But for some reason, it makes you feel sad. Does it make you want to reassess your own life? It must be embarrassing to have no husband. Is that the reason why you stopped posting comments and photos to your WeChat Circle? Or is there another reason, like you suspect some strangers are reading your posts and spying on you, which is obviously not the case.

In reply, you tap out a message explaining how you don't want to marry a Qinese man, and that you have a crush on a foreign teacher. You tell her about your job at Su'ke, and how you met Steve. You also say that you feel like someone is spying on you, and that you don't feel safe. What a silly message, Little Comrade, it's better if she never reads it.

"Stop writing to me, I don't like you," you type out.

But, Little Comrade, your messages disappear. The moment you press send, the screen flickers and you've lost your message. How odd!

"I think my phone's broken," you say.

"Who's that?" Bo Bo asks.

"It's Apple, my old bunkmate. Remember her?"

"Is she the one that got married? What a sellout."

Bo Bo's foul language and alternative lifestyle is hard to accept. Better not pay attention to her. At least she has some tea, and when it is ready she pours it for you, using her cherished tea set. Take little sips, dear Little Comrade. Don't burn your tongue.

"Heh, I love this tea set. I bought it two weeks ago," says Bo Bo. "Know where I got it? In the mall we went to today. It was a bargain, just fifty yuan. The guy I was with wouldn't buy it for me, what a cheap ass! I had to pay for it with my own money. So you think you'll come work at the KTV? You can make a lot more than Su'ke."

The idea appeals to you somewhat. You've gotten restless at the restaurant.

Also, it's been so long since you talked to your parents, and you know by the way they don't call you anymore that they are ashamed of you. You want to make them proud. You want to become rich, to show them you are worthy of their love. Trapped in your own web of deceit, that's you.

"What exactly do you do there, anyway?" you ask.

"You'll see, heh heh. You can make two hundred a night just talking and sitting. It's easy."

"Really? I don't believe it. If you made that much, you'd be living in a hotel with servants kissing your feet."

"I don't go to work every night, silly. Only when I feel like it. Anyway, it's unpredictable and you can't do it like a regular job otherwise you'd burn out. Besides, I put everything I make in the bank. I'm not going to waste good money renting a fancy apartment when this one has everything I need."

"Okay. That makes sense. Maybe I'll come try it."

"Do you have any nicer clothes? You have to wear high heels. You'll get a lot of clients. We're young, they always like the younger ones."

"All right. If I come with you to the KTV, can I try it for just one night? If I don't like it, I'll keep my job waitressing."

"Yeah, of course," she says.

# XXIII. PATRONIZE
# SMALL BUSINESSES

The next day you bring some nice clothes and high heels to the restaurant. After work Bo Bo is waiting for you.

"The KTV's just down this road. It's not far from South Flower Garden. But we can do our makeup over here."

The makeup shop you go to is a humble little shop with a sliding glass door, on a crooked alleyway known as "makeup alley." There are many such shops to be found here. The pedestrian flow is moderate, because the alleyway serves as a passage from a large main road to the back entrance of an old residential community.

As you follow Bo Bo, you see, through the cheap sliding glass doors, that in each shop there are many young women sitting in chairs, getting their makeup done before they leave to wherever they are headed. Probably they are, like you, going to the KTV to hustle up some money.

The shops are embedded in the one- or two-floor crumbling brick houses that line the uneven path. Some of these houses are in the process of being torn down. Even as they are being demolished, the inhabitants are still living there, growing vegetables in Styrofoam boxes or in the dirt, between piles of rubble. They are older folk, old grannies and grandpas with their teeth missing, with shrunken, shrivelled bodies. You, too, if you are lucky, dear Little Comrade, will look like them one day.

"This whole block will be gone soon," Bo Bo says. "I don't know where all these makeup shops will go. I'd do my own makeup but damn it's hard. I can't do a good job of it. I don't know how. Look, I've got no eyebrows at all. See? Maybe I'll get some eyebrow tattoos. Here we are."

The tiny shop is raised on a concrete step. Bo Bo slides the plastic-framed glass door to one side. A large woman, the proprietress, is attending to two young women sitting in barber chairs facing the mirrored cabinet against the wall.

The proprietress cuts hair during the day for whatever customers she may have. But toward evening young women all come to do their makeup. She adorns these female customers with fake eyelashes, with cosmetic contacts, with hair extensions and powder and foundation and a dozen other things that pretty young women need to look the way they want. The mirrored cabinet has display cases, which are full of disordered jewellery like necklaces, earrings, bracelets – any imaginable item that can be turned into a woman's accessory.

"How's business lately, madam boss?" Bo Bo says, as she sits down on a lumpy couch.

"Not so bad," says the proprietress.

As if on cue, a customer selects a pair of earrings from the mess on the mirrored cabinet and tries them on. The customer inspects herself in the mirror, turning her head side to side. "How much are these, madam boss?" she asks.

"I'll give them to you for thirty. Plus your hair and nails, that's fifty, okay?"

"Madam boss, that's too expensive, you should give me a better deal."

"It's a good deal, it really is. Those are the nicest earrings I have. Someone wanted them yesterday, but I wouldn't sell them for sixty. But you're an old customer, so I'll give them to you as a bargain." The large proprietress manoeuvres her waist to get around the shop to accept the payment.

"Yeah, okay," says the customer. She prims her hair a final time in the mirror, then turns to pay the proprietress. She steps outside carefully on her high heels, down the step, wearing the newly purchased earrings.

"This is my friend," Bo Bo says. "It's her first time working at the KTV, so I wanted to get her ready."

"She's pretty," the proprietress says, looking at you, as you get into the barber chair.

"Thanks," you say. "I'm not used to wearing much makeup."

"I'll just do a 'light' makeup job on you," says the proprietress. She has already begun padding your nose and applying makeup on your face. Behind you Bo Bo picks some wigs from the shelf at the back of the tiny, cluttered shop and tries them on.

"I'd wear these wigs, but they're so damn itchy," Bo Bo says. "I bet I could make a lot more wearing one of these. My hair's too short. The men always choose the girls with the longest cut."

"You can borrow it," says the large woman.

"Nah." Bo Bo shakes her head. "What's the point of having fake hair? It looks too strange. It falls right off if you tug it."

When the makeup has been applied, you look like a ghost in the mirror. Solid dark eyebrows stretch across your forehead. Your lips are blood-red, like you ate a red passion fruit.

"You look good," Bo Bo says. "Come on, it's my turn. Stop staring at yourself and get out of the chair. Time is money."

# XXIV. BE CAUTIOUS DURING EVENING OUTINGS

Bo Bo finishes and soon both of you are walking back out of the alleyway and onto the main road. You both look almost cartoonish with the heavy layer of makeup on your faces, but you feel confident at least. As you walk, Bo Bo gives you some tips.

"Just make them laugh, that's the whole thing. Make sure they have fun. If they like talking, listen. If they want to drink, drink with them. If they want to dance, you dance. If he wants to touch, okay no big deal. See, it's simple. Most of the time it's just chatting and carrying the conversation. That's how I learned to talk so much, in these KTVs. I'm good with these kinds of guys; I can always make them laugh. Be interesting; make them feel like a hero. You can't just sit there in his lap and look sad. He won't buy a lot of drinks and you won't get a big tip. If you want to drink alcohol, just drink as much as you want. The more the better. That's the whole point. Get them to spend as much as possible. If we get separated into different rooms, don't worry. Just do what the other girls do. Here we are."

Bo Bo pulls open a frosted glass door. It's a KTV that you've passed many times walking this street. One that you hardly noticed before. Behind the frosted door is a lounge and bar, dimly lit. A couple of women are sitting there. Bo Bo walks by without looking at them. She takes you through to the back, where she sticks her head into a backroom.

You hear her laugh and make some rude jokes to someone inside. A few moments later a man pushes the door back, looks at you and grunts.

"Now we just sit at the bar," says Bo Bo. "When a client comes in, we'll chat with him if he looks friendly. Follow my lead."

It's a slow night, it's a weekday after all. Eventually four middle-aged men in suits show up, drunk and red-faced. Bo Bo goes easily right up to one of them and starts chatting him up.

A few minutes later, Bo Bo prods you. "Come on, you. Let's go upstairs."

The four men follow behind, with another two of your new coworkers bringing up the rear.

Upstairs, the karaoke rooms are furnished with purple plush velvet sofas, lush pink carpeting and white panelled walls. It looks quite like what in "America" is commonly referred to among the younger generations as a "pimp's living room." The lighting is soft and gentle. The curtains are thick and luxurious. The decor is exquisite. The roomy generosity of the place makes you want to never leave. Built into the wall is a gigantic plasma TV.

Too bad you cannot stay here forever. Eventually you will have to go. But for now, while you are here, you partake in the activities. You are Bo Bo's "wingman." She leads, you assist. With the aid of her valuable social skills and a seemingly endless supply of Blue Sky gin, the evening passes in a blur.

Lucky for you, the men are easily pleased. Whatever you do, they think it is a "riot." Whatever you say makes them chortle until they are red with delight. But, no, wait, that is the alcohol that is making them red. But no matter, they are having fun. They compliment you on your outfit. They praise you and drink to your health. No one has ever drunk to your health before; you are beside yourself with joy. Then, after much boisterous laughter, they turn to themselves, laughing, joking, insulting each other with what might be described as uncontrollable mirth. The room is so full of second-hand smoke that you can hardly breathe, but somehow it doesn't bother you anymore. You are talking with Bo Bo and your other two coworkers, who seem to have transformed themselves into your best friends and dearest cousins. One of the men throws his arm around you and squeezes you joyfully, while another pats you on the rump. Bo Bo is up on her feet, dancing, squirming, jiggling for all she is worth in the lap of the third man. Your other two coworkers are babying the fourth, in the corner, much to the satisfaction of his wildest dreams. The music is so loud that you can't hear what anyone is saying. You drink so much that you have to go to the bathroom again and again.

But all happy times must come to an end. When you look at your phone, you discover that it's well past one in the morning. The men have left. The party is over. Two of your coworkers have departed with the four nice gentlemen, though you don't know where to. Downstairs, on the first floor, Bo Bo collects some cash from the backroom. Two hundred for you, two hundred for Bo Bo.

"What did I tell you? That was easy, wasn't it?" she says. Bo Bo is a little tipsy. She manages to walk straight, however. "See how much money is just floating around? There are rich businessmen everywhere. They blow a couple thousand a night like it's small change. It's a business expense for them, rubbing the backs of city officials and clients. They have a client, and they want to show the client a good time. So they go to the KTV. They hang out and get drunk. It's good for business. They get loosened up and become buddies. That's how the men are. In the office, they can't relax. They're too uptight to close a deal. They have to get drunk over dinner and go to the KTV together. You know, hire a few girls to do the pampering. Then the deal is sealed. So why not just work at the KTV. It's just part of the new capitalist system, right or right? Meanwhile everyone else is scrounging for crumbs. My stomach hurts." She grabs her belly. She pukes into the bushes.

"Come on," you say, "let's go home. You need to get into bed."

# XXV. HONOUR BUSINESS AGREEMENTS

And so you adjust to your new routine. Over the next week you quit your job at Manager Mu's restaurant and instead begin working regularly at the KTV.

One weekend, Bo Bo suggests taking a break. "It feels good to have money, doesn't it? Should we go to the KTV tonight and make some more cash? Or should we go to the foot massage instead? I like to go to Tong Massage, the wooden foot bath. We can get two young guys to massage our feet. Maybe we can get an extra service, like have the toenail and foot master clean our feet."

"Nah, it's too expensive," you say.

"Yeah, okay. We can go to the KTV tonight, and then do the foot massage tomorrow. Sunday, the day of rest and relaxation." Bo Bo throws her hands behind her head and enthusiastically sighs. "When I get rich, I'm gonna go to the spas every day. I love ordering them to massage my feet and everything. Sitting in the chair like I'm the wife of some big boss. That's my dream. Marry a rich Taiwanese business mogul. Let's see if people give me attitude then. I hate being poor and everyone treating me like dirt. I can't wait to have the tables turned, then I'll laugh for the rest of my life."

That night you and Bo Bo dress and get made up and go to the KTV. Unlike when you first started out in the KTV, you aren't so nervous any more. You even feel a little cocky and self-assured. You tell yourself that you are one of the group, the "in-crowd." You know what goes on behind the frosted doors, and it's nothing that you can't handle.

"It's Saturday, it'll be busy," warns Bo Bo. "We should be able to make a lot tonight. Plenty of business, but lots of girls too. Heh heh, so many pretty girls in this city. All pretty 'missies.'"

The street is alive with people. Inside the KTV a dozen young women come and go, all made up, all pretty like so many gift-wrapped boxes. Almost right away Bo Bo gets shepherded into a group and sent upstairs. She waves to you as she disappears. Wave goodbye to your friend, dear Little Comrade. You are on your own.

A moment later, you join a group of two other young women. Along with three men, you find yourself in a room on the second floor, drinking and being merry.

The other hostesses are enthusiastic dancers, although they're not so much dancing as gyrating and wiggling. A tray of alcohol arrives. The men become increasingly drunk. In the low light, the other hostesses rub up to the men and are fondled. The man you are with does the same to you. At first you resist a little, but then, quite effortlessly, you stop resisting. It seems pointless to you now. You sit back in the plush sofa and let him grope as he likes.

How does it feel, Little Comrade, to have a drunken man's hands on your body?

But wait. Your eyes are closed. You notice there is no more groping.

Open your eyes. What do you see? Two of the men are helping a third out of the room. The third one has passed out from excessive drinking. They stumble down the stairs. They are gone. Downstairs you look for Bo Bo, but she is nowhere to be found.

The next group of men come. To your surprise, you recognize one of them. It is Q, your former coworker. Your former "flame." He looks much older, much more worn, since you last saw him. He is fatter around the neck and waist. He's flush from drinking too much alcohol. Still, afraid that he will spot you and recognize you, you try to hurry away.

"Hello! You," he says, and snatches you by the wrist before you can abscond. "Is that my ex-girlfriend? Yes, I thought so. I didn't recognize you at first, with all your makeup on. But you look so pretty now, even prettier than before. Come on, let's have a reunion!" He slumps his arm over your shoulder. His mouth, a few inches from yours, smells like ashtrays and gym shoes.

Escape, dear Little Comrade, while you can! But, alas, you cannot escape. There is nowhere to go, and this is where you belong. A tall, thin, witch of a woman, Madam Boss, the establishment's proprietress, watches as you proceed upstairs to begin a new party, to make another palmful of cash.

As before there is singing and jostling and much general merriment. The other hostesses compete and outdo each other. The music thumps above all else. Q has one hand on your buttocks, and another hand on your chest. He is making up for lost time.

"So where do you want to go after?" he breathes into your face. You can taste the flecks of saliva that eject from his mouth into yours. You try to be a good hostess and ignore it.

"Well, I'm tired, I'll probably go home," you say.

"Home." Q bursts out in riotous laughter, rocking you on his knee. "Where's that, pretty missy? Not the factory, after all. Ever since you left the factory, I've been disappointed. Now, how lucky I am to accidentally stumble on you. I won't let you out of my sight this time. I can walk you home after, how about that? Maybe I can come in for a drink too."

He calls you "missy" because, after all, that's what the hostesses are, no?

"My home's very poor," you say. "It's just a small room, there's nowhere to drink. You wouldn't like it."

"Well, we can go to a hotel then, pretty missy. I have a hotel room for the weekend, it's the White Swan Hotel, it's a four-star hotel, very comfortable I promise."

"That's nice. But I really have to go home after with my friend."

"Rubbish," Q says. He buries his face in your chest. You pull on his balding head to get the big animal away from you, but it is futile.

Bo Bo is not in the room. Where is she? When you can, you stick your head out of the KTV room. You look down the hall, but she is not there. With the loud music, the drunken singing, the random strangers and hostesses walking in and out, it's too confusing. No one knows who you are. No one knows who you are looking for. You call her phone; you send her a text and a WeChat message. But there's no reply.

"Come, it's getting late," Q says. He staggers to his feet. His friends have taken the other hostesses by their slim wrists. Some are more willing than others. Some are excited, some are indifferent. Madam Boss is there at the bottom of the staircase.

Q pulls you along. "I can't go with you, I'm really sorry," you mumble.

"Hey, what's your name?" says Madam Boss to you. "I'm the owner of this joint, so you do what I say. Go on, you'll have a good time."

"I can't, I'm waiting for Bo Bo."

Unfortunately, the protesting does little to change Madam Boss's mind. She holds you by the arm, pulls you over to the corner. "What do you think you're doing?" she says. "You want to ruin my business? Go with that man. He's a customer and he paid good money. You think you can tell me I can't decide what to do in my own shop? You want me to have you arrested for trespassing? For theft? Go on, you'll get your cut, don't worry about that. Just stop fussing so much. He wants you. He's a handsome guy; go make him happy. Whoever heard of a missy turning down a deal?" She forces you into Q's arms. He bundles you up and shuffles you outside.

You manage to yank your arm away and walk, crossing the street. All you can think about is getting home. Go on then, Little Comrade, see if Bo Bo is in her room, she will protect you.

"Where are you going?" says Q. He walks after you, but you can only ignore him.

"I need to go home." On your phone, you call Bo Bo again and again, but she doesn't pick up.

"Is this where you live?" says Q.

"Yeah, why?" you say.

"Guess it's better than living in B Dorm. It's a nice community here. I like this street. Lots of places to eat. Am I right? Heh, well, you might look down on me, but I don't live in B Dorm any more either. You think just because I work at the factory that I'm poor, right? No, I got promoted, I'm a manager now. See, you wasted your life. You wasted your chance, now look at you, missy."

You see Bo Bo's room, number 42 faded above. The narrow window is closed, and the curtain is drawn. You can tell the light is off and there's no one home.

"Is this your room?" says Q.

"No, it's my friend's."

"Why don't you show me your room? I won't do anything; I just want to have a drink of tea. I'm thirsty. Then I'll be on my way. I'm tired too."

"All right, but you have to promise, okay?"

"I promise," says Q, with a chuckle. "You're so cute, that's why you attract me, so innocent."

You open the door to the room adjacent to Bo Bo's. There's nothing to do but put on some tea. Soon you are sitting on your bed and the tea is boiling. Q comes in and closes the door behind him. The room is so cramped that there is nowhere to turn. Nowhere to hide except under the blankets.

"Such a pretty girl, a pretty face. You must have a lot of boys chasing after you these days. You'll be married soon, I bet. Why not have some fun before that happens?"

"I'm saving myself for someone special," you say.

"I'm not special?" says Q.

"I have a boyfriend, he's a foreigner. He's from America," you say.

Q chokes with laughter. "That's a good one, great. He treats you really well. Having you work in the KTV bar! Come here, let me put my arm around you. I won't hurt you. You were so nice in the bar, why be sour now? I like sweet. Sweet pretty missy."

"Stop it!" you say.

"Hey, I paid for you," he says. "I paid your madam already. So I'm going to do what I paid for, you no good thief."

You try to move away, but there's only the wall. Look at the wall, dear Little Comrade! Look. What do you see? You see the beautiful, handsome face of "Ryan Reynolds." The powerful image helps you endure what is happening.

Q has his hand up your dress. Your undergarments are off. It all happens in a blur. He drops you on the bed like a rag doll and shudders over you in a few quick spasms.

Keep looking at the wall. Don't look at Q. When he is done, your eyes are blank.

Q is already finished. He stares at you for a moment. Then he pushes himself back upright. He is on his feet. He pulls up his pants and with a neat click, buckles them.

"What's the matter with you?" he says. He cannot take his eyes off your expressionless face. He slaps you on the cheek firmly. You don't respond. Still, you are staring at the wall. Visualization is a key strategy to promoting morale.

A voice is talking to you. You cannot ignore it forever.

"Don't you speak anymore?" says Q. "Didn't you like it? You little missy slut. Say something. All you missies are the same. Don't even know how to have a good time in bed. You're just as bad as you were last time. What a waste of money."

He shakes his head and mutters to himself. He quickly reaches into his pocket and pulls out some red bills. He throws three of them on your lifeless body.

"There, don't say I wasn't fair," he says. "That's a tip. That's more than what I normally give. I shouldn't give you anything, but I'm a nice guy."

He opens the door and then is gone.

# XXVI. RECOGNIZE
# YOUR FAILINGS

You are in the same clothes, curled up with the blanket around you. It is the next day. Having no place to shower, you lie there in your bed the whole night. Your body feels like it is bloated, filled with poison, festering with insects, rotting and decaying.

Bo Bo knocks on your door. She knows you are inside. She can see you through the window. When you prop it open, you see she has a takeout lunch, an order of rice noodles and soup and an assortment of small containers holding salty egg, seaweed and other fine items.

"There you are," she says. She thrusts the tray of food in, and holds up her other hand, a wad of red bills in it.

"Madam Boss gave this to me for you. She said you made it last night. Heh, look at this. You must have made a good impression on her. I wanted to go out for lunch to celebrate, but I was so hungry. I couldn't wait for you to wake up, so I ordered something for both of us."

Go on, dear Little Comrade, tell your friend what happened. It's okay, you can. You open your mouth to say it, but the words get stuck in your throat. It's impossible to say such a shameful thing out loud. Only now do you learn, Little Comrade.

"Aren't you hungry?" Bo Bo says. She's eating, but she stops. "Hey, tell me, what happened?"

You begin to cry. You tuck your head into your chest and you begin to sob. You curl up into a ball; you cry uncontrollably. Let it out, dear Little Comrade. Your whole body quivers and shakes. You want to kill yourself; you want the whole world, every object in the planet to collapse into you. To destroy you, to obliterate you from existence.

Bo Bo jumps up from her squat where she was eating from a bowl.

"Hey, hey," she says. "Crap! I knew something was wrong." You hold on to her, but it's no use, you keep shivering and crying. She is your friend, but she does not know what to do. "Those assholes, I knew it," she says. "I hate that Madam Boss. I thought something was up. Listen, don't cry. We won't go there any more, okay? We don't need to go to that place. Goddamn it, there's too many perverts and lowlifes in this city. I shouldn't have left you alone."

You hug her. Before long, however, Bo Bo is again squatting on the floor. She must eat, she is hungry. To her it is just another day at the office. Another day at work, an occupational hazard.

"Come on, eat something before it gets cold," she says. "Look, I bought a subscription to PPTV. Now we can get all these movies unlocked. Good idea, huh? What do you want to see? How about some 'American' movies."

"No," you say. "I don't want to watch those." For some reason, just hearing the word *American* makes you sick to your stomach. Just the thought of seeing a photo of "Ryan Reynolds" makes you ill. You have created an emotional link between the "American" symbol and the experience of being raped.

Don't feel bad about it, Little Comrade, that feeling is a sign of progress and patriotic maturity.

Bo Bo ignores your answer, however, and scrolls down the list of movies under the "American" heading. She picks one at random. "This one looks fun," she says.

The two of you lie in bed. It is late afternoon. You watch an old, strange movie called *American Beauty* on Bo Bo's phone. The scenery, the people, the sounds that come out of the characters' mouths – it all makes you feel nauseated. The lead character, a balding white man who speaks with a lisp, looks like a pedophile and rapist.

"This movie reminds me of that what's his face we saw at the English centre," Bo Bo says. "That Qinese guy pretending to be from America. Mark, right? He spoke English like these people do."

You can't really recall how Mark spoke, nor does it seem to matter much to you.

"Come on, you can't lie there all day feeling sorry for yourself," Bo Bo says. "What you need is someone nice, someone who will treat you better. Why don't we go talk to that teacher? It'll cheer you up, won't it? You can forget about all these petty problems. Look at me, I'm a loser here, me and Madam Boss and the rest of those goons. You're better than this. One day you'll travel the world and see it all, and I'll still be living in this closet. Madam Boss will still be shovelling feces out of the toilet."

"Do you think he'd really talk to me?" you say.

"Of course, didn't you see how he was looking at us that night? He had his eyeballs all over you. I bet he'd drool like a lapdog if you so much as winked at him. Anyway, what's the harm in trying? Believe me, I had the same thing happen to me too, some guy put a date-rape drug in my drink and you know what happened. The first thing I did the next day was find a new guy who drooled all over me and followed me around like a pet. It'll make you feel better. Why don't we go over there right now?"

You shake your head and roll away from the screen. The movie is still playing on Bo Bo's phone. Just the thought of men, and of "America," makes you sick.

# PART THREE

# XXVII. TURN YOUR LIFE AROUND

Even with Bo Bo comforting you, the trauma is still there. At night the shame burns in your chest and between your legs. Is it shame or something else? Certainly not a transmitted disease spreading pus and ooze inside your private organs, right? Now that you are a soiled woman, there's no future for you.

You may dream of Steve, but now that you have been used, Steve will have nothing to do with you. What options do you have? You search your mind furiously. Short of jumping off a building roof, how else can you redeem yourself? What about that nice boy back on Chongming Island? Your best bet is to settle for Wang Dong, but even Wang Dong may not take you now.

Little Comrade, there are a few points to consider. First, you're no longer what might pass for a "fresh" woman. That's to say, even though your first night romantically involved with a man didn't go as hoped, for better or worse the physical act happened. No denying that.

Maybe it's for the best that you were taken advantage of by Q, a sort of wake-up call to spur you off your misguided path.

In the morning, as you make your way to the train station, keep your life in perspective. Looking for the right life partner is a challenge. You took your shot and failed. Let someone with more experience handle your affairs. Who better than your mother? She can answer all the questions you have pertaining to the opposite gender, and the project of baby making.

Having made up your mind, you feel relief. Almost yesterday you took the same trip. Only, your life is so different now. If you feel nervous, distract yourself by looking around.

There are two train stations in the city. One old station for regular trains, like K trains and D trains, which have been in operation for decades. Across the street is the new station for bullet trains, which use high-speed rail. The bullet train system is the crowning achievement of our transportation system, which continues to expand relentlessly to every corner of the country.

The station is bustling with crowds. It's easy to buy tickets. Head over to the automated ticket machine, press a button, swipe your identity and payment card. The ticket pops out like magic. That is the work of our country's best engineers. Put your bag on the X-ray machine. Gather at Gate 3 for a bullet train to Shanghai.

The train arrives. So sleek, it slides along the platform edge like a metallic eel. Before you board the train, take a moment to thank your government.

Aboard, your ticket entitles you to a seat in one of the plush chairs on either side of the aisle. Sit down, enjoy the view.

Unfortunately, the seats are cramped. The passenger in front of you reclines his seat, squeezing you even more.

Behind you is a mother with her child. The child, three or four years old, is acting up. He is something of a "little emperor," an only child spoiled beyond any reasonable measure. His mother pays no mind as he kicks and throws his body in an annoying fashion at the back of your seat. You bounce forward, and your head jiggles every three seconds. You turn around to scowl at the mother, who is chatting with her friend seated next to her. The child has no seat of his own. He cannot sit still so it does not matter. The mother reprimands her child, but in a half-hearted way, which the boy dutifully ignores.

Dear Little Comrade, don't be too upset at this "little emperor." After all, aren't you yourself just like him? With your insistence that you are special? Admit it, you once believed you deserved a foreign man different from the Qinese man nature intended you to fall in love with. In fact, you were a "little empress." But, fortunately, this kind of thinking was only a phase in your life. Now you have grown out of it, just like this boy will grow out of his.

On the train, your phone beeps. Apple has just sent you a message, telling you how happy she is.

"I thought I blacklisted Apple from my WeChat," you say. "So strange."

Odd indeed, almost as if some higher force has tampered with your account and changed the settings. Impossible, right? Little Comrade, you'd be impressed by what some of the best technologists in our country can do.

As much as her text fills you with mixed emotion, shouldn't you reply to Apple?

Take a moment to compose a reply. No point in wondering why she never got your last note. Instead try to come up with a better message this time, one that has a better chance of finding its way into her inbox.

Dear Apple,

You were right all along. I plan on marrying Wang Dong. I want to invite you to the wedding even though you are so far away. It will mean a lot if you can come. I miss you so much and I'm so glad that everything is working out for you.

Your loving friend, Little Comrade

Your fingers feel stiff, almost like they are moving against their will. But take a deep breath. Now that you have made up your mind, it's easy sailing.

That's all it takes. One little note will set off a chain of events that will usher in your new, perfect life. But did you just spit at your phone? Why did you do that? Or was that a sneeze?

It might interest you to know, Little Comrade, that the camera on your phone is always on, even when you think your phone is off. Always behave as if someone is watching you, isn't that something every mother tells her child?

Perhaps you are frustrated. Online, you post about certain topics or say things that you should not say. When you look again at your microblogging posts they are missing, those posts where you said some uncharacteristically bad things. Inexplicable, isn't it? As if someone somewhere is monitoring what you say online and deleting all your bad comments on your behalf. How preposterous your paranoia is! This uncertainty makes you nauseated and want to avoid social media altogether. Too bad, Little Comrade, your loss.

The fact is, the only way to stop this constant pressure to get married is . . . simply to get married, right? A stable future caring for a traditional Qinese man. Why did you punch the back of the chair in front of you, Little Comrade?

Instead of sulking, pick Wang Dong or Q, either one of these gentlemen who have been trying to win your affection.

Go ahead, pick the one that is most palatable to you, the least irksome. You're free to choose, you have as much freedom here as anywhere else, including "America." Who is the handsomer and more acceptable of the two? Q or Dong? Consider the pros and cons.

First, Q. You have known Q longer. He is your childhood sweetheart, in a sense. Your "first." Sure, he did something or other to you in bed, once or twice. But it was over quickly, with no lasting ill effects. And aren't you at least partly responsible? After all, you worked in such a place, seducing men for a living. He was the victim of your enticements. Any man would have behaved similarly. However, Q's reliability as a husband, as a homemaker, may be questionable.

Now for Dong. Despite Dong's awkward, nerdy nature, compared to Q he's not that bad, is he? He's a good man at heart, with innocent ambitions – a simple desire to wed you, to have you care for him into old age and most of all to impregnate you with a baby boy so his family name can live on and honour can come to him and his parents. Lucky you!

True, Dong may be lacking in social skills, and falling in love with him is difficult. But that is to be expected from young people who, through no fault of their own, have spent too little time in real face-to-face interactions. Their experiences are limited to the digital "meta" universe. That is not something you should hold against him.

Just remember your own predicament. "Par for the course," to use a saying from "America."

# XXVIII. TAKE ADVANTAGE OF PARENTS' HOSPITALITY

Over the next week, you find yourself on the outskirts of Chongming Island. During the day, you help your parents with their convenience shop. At night, you sleep in a shack attached to their brick home.

Presently your mother is in a closet space at the back of the shop, chopping vegetables and preparing meat. She rinses rice in a bucket, saving the water. She will use the water to wash vegetables, meat and then, after dinner, the dishes. Your mother is wise, she knows the starch from the rice is good for absorbing bad and oily residue.

Look at your mother, Little Comrade. See how she observes her wifely duties. Do you see yourself in her? She married your father when she was two years younger than you are now. Why wait for a role model when you have the perfect one right in front of you?

For lunch, mother, father and child sit on footstools on the sidewalk. This is where your parents eat every day, so that they don't have to close shop. Your father eats with his head down, hardly stopping to breathe.

Conversation revolves around your father's business, the little shop. As the meal ends, however, the subject turns to your plight.

"Daughter," says your mother, "you need to take life seriously and marry. What about Wang Dong? I thought you liked him."

"Mother is right," says your father.

Do you want to respond? Why sit mute with a scowl on your face? You came back home, so why not accept your fate?

"Look at these gifts the Wangs sent you. This is from little Dong." Your mother shows you a brand-new dress, gift-wrapped and delivered from Taobao.

Was there a time when you joked with your father over dinner? Perhaps long ago. With each passing day unmarried, you become a disgrace and burden upon the family. What can your father say in the face of such failure? At the front of everyone's mind is this whole problem of finding someone willing to marry you, so that you can finally have a baby boy and redeem yourself.

When the food is eaten, your mother clears the plates. Your father looks expectantly, clacking his tongue to signal you to help. In the back of the shop, in the closet sink, she rinses them with the leftover water from washing rice. This is the chance for you to show what a grateful child you are by helping. Instead, you sit there shaking your head. No one knows why you are shaking your head.

"Good meal," says your father. "Maodou beans are better than last year."

Your parents cook the food you like. Spicy style, extra salty. Free meals in your hometown every day without lifting a finger.

After lunch, your mother kindly takes you to visit your soon-to-be fiancé, Wang Dong.

You find him in his mother's apartment. Like last time, he is dressed in something akin to pajamas. But compared to last visit's hurried glance, this time you have all the time to look. He is a slim young man, greasy black hair, wearing slippers and brown sleeping pants and shirt. He slouches in front of a big, old computer, clicking rapidly on a mouse, smoking a cigarette. He glances over at you and waves.

"What game are you playing?" you ask.

"Trying to win a chicken dinner, what else?"

Before you were sure there was no chemistry. But now, with one final tap of the mouse, he pauses his game and looks at you, a glint of lechery in his eye. You have to start somewhere, Little Comrade.

Aren't you looking forward to your new life? You will be, if not happy, at least free from bodily harm. Isn't that more than anyone like you can ask for?

Be polite, make an effort. His personality, his looks are not all that bad. He has a job involving phone and emailing campaigns, an illegitimate enterprise but an enterprise nonetheless. Best of all, his family is close to your family. After you marry, you can still spend lots of time with your mother and father.

"Thanks for sending the gifts," you say.

"What gifts?"

"The dress."

"Oh, yeah. I guess." He coughs up some phlegm and noisily expectorates into a floor pan. He likes you, it's clear, but he's pretending to be disinterested. That's what all cool guys do.

"Are you okay, do you need some water?" you ask. Good, like a normal woman, you exhibit a high degree of empathy and caring for the male species.

After producing more expectorate, Dong leans back into his chair. He lights up another cigarette. You can feel his eyes moving up and down your body, trying to judge your physical appearance underneath your clothing. To be frank, there is a dull disappointment in his eyes.

Discreetly he looks at the photo of you on his phone, saved from your WeChat Circle. The truth is, he doesn't recognize you. In the photos in your WeChat Circle, your face is airbrushed and filtered so much. Isn't it a sign of the times when a man cannot even recognize the woman he is courting?

Will you take him as your husband or not, Little Comrade? Perhaps it's best for someone like you, someone with no morals, to fall in love with a foreigner and marry abroad, so that we can be rid of your bad ways and influence.

"So how have you been?" you say to Wang Dong.

"Okay."

That's the spirit, Little Comrade. Even though you are used goods, some men are still interested. Why this is probably can be explained through biology or economic class theory. Anyway, you have skinny duck legs, a skinny torso and an A-cup bra, so what's the big attraction, it's hard to say. At least your face is pretty, if oily.

"Let's give them some time alone," your mother says.

Sitting with Dong, with the afternoon light streaming in, you can feel the proximity of his body. His physique may be dwarfish compared with a foreign man, but he has the advantage of thousands of years of Qinese culture, which informs his mentality. He knows best how to treat you. Isn't that better than a hairy foreign man? How can any foreign man compete with that?

Don't forget, the Wangs are well off and can afford a monetary gift on your wedding day. Your parents need the money for your younger brother.

Just like nature intended, it's common for families to have an older daughter, little brother pairing. When a daughter is born, parents know they have failed and must try until they have a boy, thus ending up with older daughter. At the same time, it's harmonious because when older daughter is married, money comes into the household, which can be used to pay a bride price so son can have a wife. What an excellent, natural societal tradition, just like the virtuous circle of yin and yang.

Now think. Who are you to disrupt this heavenly cycle? Where will your brother's tuition come from? Will it sprout from the mountainside? Don't put yourself first when so many others are counting on you.

"I don't mind getting married," Dong says. "As long as the bride price isn't too high. When do you want to have the wedding?" He stubs out the cigarette and blows smoke in your direction. His teeth may be crooked and discoloured, but if you take the time to count them, they're all there.

# XXIX. ENJOY PEACEFUL TIME WITH PARENTS

In the morning you have breakfast. So delicious – fried rice noodles, boiled eggs, spicy seaweed, corn nib soup with peanuts and white carrot. Then you go with Wang Dong to the grocery store where he buys two cases of yoghurt. Gifts for your parents.

"Get two bottles of rice alcohol as well," you say.

Dong inspects the price tag. "These are too expensive."

You don't mind getting cheap bottles, but the cheap ones don't come with a gift bag. "We're buying a nice bottle," you tell the sales helper, showing her an expensive bottle. However, at the cashier, you hide the expensive bottle and have the cashier ring up the cheap one, while keeping the nice bag.

The saleswoman catches on and hurries over. You rush out of the store after having paid, clutching the bottle and gift bag to your small bosom. They yell after you and your husband-to-be, but since they are old, frumpy aunties, they cannot catch you. Close call, Little Comrade, you have a habit of taking too many risks.

Inside your father's shop, your mother works in a red apron. Your father is busy unloading inventory from his flatbed truck. Your grandmother sits on an upturned crate, peeling maodou beans and scrubbing duck eggs.

Nobody fusses over you. For one, you're soon to be married, soon to belong to another family. Also, where's your son? Yet to produce a son. Once you have done that, your parents, relatives, neighbours will flock around whenever you show up.

"Finally, getting married. I can die in peace now," says your mother. She shakes her head, pursing her lips.

Your parents make a show over Wang Dong, perhaps because of the gifts and the possibility of a generous bride price. They pat him on the back, they make him feel welcomed. Perhaps he will even invest a few yuan into your father's convenience store.

Now that Wang Dong is here beside you, old aunties, uncles and grannies stop to chitchat. Enjoy this prelude to a lifetime of harmony and togetherness,

Little Comrade. Other curious passersby on the road look in your direction, their hands behind their backs, lower lips jutting out, inscrutable expressions on their faces. The simple ones scratch their heads and blurt out, "Who's that?"

"My fiancé," you reply.

Hopefully things will work out. If not, you'll be a disgrace and banished from your parents' home. All the neighbours will gossip and snicker about how your man has abandoned you, how your family is full of fools.

At the store, an older woman drops by to purchase a watermelon. A granny wants some chicken soup base. This part of Chongming Island is where old people come to retire, living easily on one-thousand-yuan pensions each month.

The sky begins to drizzle. You walk past a few stores to a shop called One Hundred Gifts, run by a man everyone calls "Handsome Big Brother." You've known him for many years. You should call him uncle because he's close to your father's age. But Handsome Big Brother is what he likes to be called.

"How much for an umbrella?"

Try out the big one, try out the small one. Like always you want to buy the cheapest. But no sense in buying a bad umbrella that will break on the first use. And besides, you are soon to be a Qinese man's wife, you are entitled to some dignity.

Early the next morning, like always, the street buzzes with activity. At the shop, your mother is boiling locally grown corn with yellow and brown nibs. It's your favourite, the mushy, chewy kind. Your grandmother is sitting on the sidewalk crate, cleaning duck eggs with steel wool and a bucket of black water.

"Go get some food for breakfast," says your mother. She sits heavily down on a wood stool, preparing to help grandmother clean duck eggs.

You get some food from the mantou, porridge and bun shop down the street. So many choices: soy milk, fried egg batter and sausage on hot plate with fried bun and sauces. You are hungry so you also get a dumpling for yourself. So greedy, Little Comrade.

An uncle drops by your father's shop.

"Eaten yet, uncle?" you say.

"I'm not 'uncle,'" says the man indignantly. "Call me 'grandpa.'"

"You're too young to be grandpa. You're the same age as my dad. If I called you grandpa, you'd be getting undue respect." This kind of jovial banter is common among old friends and makes you feel at home.

"Your dad is fifty, right? Well, I'm sixty. That means it's 'grandpa.'"

"Only ten years older? That's too much honour. Same generation as my father, so it's more like 'uncle.'"

This kind of comradeship and happy banter wouldn't be possible if your family was covered with shame. Since everyone knows you are about to be married, everyone can relax and have fun. With a husband, at least you are not a discarded woman, an over-the-hill shrew. You have escaped the fate of those lonely single women of child-bearing age.

In the morning, your brother groggily washes his face in the shop's closet sink. He arrived from a nearby city where he has been loafing for the last year. Somehow, he has a paper cut on his finger, perhaps a splinter. His soft hands are so delicate, and you chide him on it.

"What a baby you are!"

"Leave me alone."

Your younger brother graduated from high school. But because of the hard university entrance exam, he couldn't get any further. Anyway, he isn't interested in exerting his intellectual muscles anymore. Unemployed, unmotivated, with few prospects, he sponges off your parents, who will soon have to pay an exorbitant amount to find a bride for him. No doubt some unlucky child of a greedy family in a neighbouring village will be the perfect match.

In your eyes, your brother is a failure. But, still, he's a boy and you're a girl, so there's really not that much to laugh about.

By the road, you sit on a stool and peel maodou beans. The pile of shells gets bigger by your feet. "Don't throw them out," your mother snaps, "someone will come by and buy these peels. They're worth good money."

Out on the dusty road, cars, scooters, rickety trucks, bicycles roll by. Two dogs trot over, with their loins connected. The smaller dog yelps. They appear to be attached at the buttocks, each facing the opposite direction. One pulls one way and the other, the other. Even you, naive as you are, know that these dogs have been up to disgusting things.

Wang Dong drops by and you go for a walk with him. Down the street, beyond a stretch of fields, is a bridge over one of the man-made water channels that slice through Chongming Island. You both take in the sun and cool breeze. Docked on the side is a boat captained by a shirtless man, holding a fishnet.

Perched on the bridge, you call out. "Hey, Jolly Chen. Look, it's me, Little Comrade."

"Oh, you!"

"He's an old family friend. Last time I saw him, he refused to help me move a gas tank. He was watching the TV we have in our shop, and I asked him for help. When he refused, I grabbed the remote from him and turned off the TV. 'Don't come around here anymore, watching our TV and using up our electricity,' I said. That guy is an 'old gramp.'"

"Old gramp?"

"You know. Guys at the park doing tai chi every morning, playing chess with other old folks, square dancing with aunties. On the bus, he'll argue over a seat. At the supermarket, he goes with a granny to haggle. He's balding down the middle with two tufts of hair, face always oily, slippers on his feet. Old gramps have a hot water bottle in one hand with red gouqi leaves in it."

Wang Dong nods his head. Little Comrade, you and your husband-to-be are settling into comfortable married life, able to share jokes with each other.

"The opposite of that is 'hot uncle.' Cool guys who wake up for a run in the morning. During the day hot uncles talk business, drink tea, play golf. Night comes and they go out with buddies, host dinners or take a jeep for a safari adventure. Hot uncles are handsome, well-dressed guys with money and rich relatives. He's the guy the girls want, you know?"

"Like me, right?" says Wang Dong. You wait for him to chuckle at his own joke, but he doesn't.

# XXX. PREPARE FOR A
# SMOOTH MARRIAGE

Over the next few days, you help your parents with the shop. Besides making change for customers, you unload supplies. When your father shows up with a truck full of watermelons, you help. Your father stands on the flatbed and hands the watermelons to you and your mother on the road, where you put them into a basket.

Hundreds of pounds of watermelons fill up baskets around the truck. The wire baskets are old and bent out of shape. The rim of each basket, the only place where you can grip, has a foam covering that is torn to pieces. It doesn't matter to your father, his hands are thick and used to labour, but because you are a woman, your hands are weak and the wire hurts you.

Instead of storing away the last basket of watermelons, you and your mother load it onto the back of a red trike near the roadside. On a scrap piece of Styrofoam you help your illiterate mother write the words *Watermelon, 30 cents per catty.*

No sooner do you erect the sign than an urban order patrol official who stands all day on the corner starts walking toward you.

The patrolman mutters as he passes, waving at the watermelons that should not be obstructing the sidewalk. You ignore him. But ten minutes later, on his way back in your direction, you hop up from your footstool and cover the watermelons with a tarp. As soon as the patrolman is gone, you uncover the watermelons. Quick thinking, Little Comrade, but try to be law-abiding. To make his day better, when you see this lanky guard, always wave and ask if he's had lunch. He's a foot soldier of our country's indispensable bureaucracy. Don't look down on him. He has a hard job to do, managing a city full of troublemakers like you.

It is nearing dinnertime. Wang Dong comes over to join you and your family. Your mother sends you to the local market.

"We need crayfish, aunty," you say.

The woman selling seafood is just about ready to get off work. She has only three piles of seafood left on her wet table. The shrimp and crayfish squirm about like little space aliens. "I'll have thirty yuan of those, aunty." Thirty yuan isn't enough to buy the whole pile. But aunty puts all the crayfish into a plastic bag and thrusts it into Wang Dong's hands. When you try to pay, she refuses money. You force the crumpled bills into her hand, but she pushes them to Wang Dong. Wang Dong stands there with the cash, unsure what to do. Aunty is a good friend. Every year, your family always gives her fruit.

"No need to be so polite," aunty says. "Enjoy the crayfish."

Finally, it's dinnertime. Wang Dong brings out the rice-filled bowls. You direct him to give the first bowl to your grandmother, the second to your father, the third to your mother. When the chopsticks are given out, you sit down on footstools, elbow to elbow, around the squat little table. This is communal dining. Everyone plunges their chopsticks willy-nilly into the food. The food is oily and spicy just the way you like. It's you, your parents, your brother, your grandmother and Wang Dong.

Your brother hunches over, rice bowl in one hand. He dips his chopsticks in each of the dishes, swirling the food. There are three shared dishes. A bean vermicelli and beef, the steamed crayfish with peppers and maodou, and a shredded hot and sour potato.

While your family is eating, a group of men and women huddle around a card table outside the barbershop. Your family ignores them, but a young girl detaches from the crowd and comes over to you, giggling and running back and forth. She holds up a phone and takes photos of you.

"What do you want?" you ask. "If you take any more photos, I'll slap you!" Everyone at your table scowls at the girl. No matter what is said to her, she is undeterred. The girl runs off and comes back with a stray dog. The dog burrows underneath the table, upsetting everyone. You scrunch your face and look up at the sky with your fists balled.

"Sister," the kid says. "You're getting married, right? How much are your parents getting? How much is the bride price? I bet I'll get more than you when the time comes."

"You're shameless. Get lost!" you shout. It's so embarrassing. Thankfully, the dog runs off, and the girl follows it.

Try to hide your embarrassment, Little Comrade. Concentrate on the crayfish. Fortunately, the taste is so delicious, it's easy to lose yourself in the meal. You suck the flavour from your chopsticks and plop the shells back into the dish. Your brother pokes his chopsticks in the plate of maodou. His chopsticks swirl the oily beans around. He picks one or two ripe beans and drops them back into the sauce, picks another and pops it into his mouth. You do the same, as does your mother. Your grandmother burps loudly; your mother spits bones onto the table. Your father throws a beer can at the stray dog that has returned and now crouches, waiting for scraps.

Such a wonderful family life. On another night, your mother makes a thick broth of corn grains and lotus seeds, and you eat wheat wraps, a local specialty of your hometown village.

"Can I have some more rice?" You hold up your bowl.

You are used to eating until your gullet is stuffed, just in case a famine is coming. You hand your mother your empty bowl and she packs a heaping amount of rice in it.

"Is that enough?" she says.

"Yeah," you say, burping, "enough."

Dig in, Little Comrade. After all, you are more or less married. It doesn't matter to anyone what you look like anymore.

After dinner you take your grandma for a walk. The dim yellow streetlights seem to make the dark night even darker. All around is the chirping of crickets. Across fields of rice stalks, dogs bark.

# XXXI. PICK A GOOD TIME FOR YOUR WEDDING

The marriage plan comes together quickly. First, Dong appears, bearing gifts, including an electric German massage pillow, which you take out and show your mother.

"You'll like this," you say. Your mother tries it out but doesn't seem to like it.

"What's wrong?" Wang Dong says.

"She likes it, she'll get used to using it later," you say.

Yes, you're low middle class. This is the life of hard-working villagers moving up in the world.

The idea is to have lunch with Dong's mother and father at a little restaurant by the river. Inside, the restaurant is crowded with customers. Wang Dong's parents are there already, and everyone falls into introductions and laughter. The owner shakes your father's hand, congratulating him on your marriage.

Your party has the only private space in the restaurant, in a bare and unfinished room, with a tiny jail-like window near the ceiling, and a fan in the corner blowing hot air.

Over the meal, Wang Dong's father and your father discuss this business of the bride price. There is some perfunctory haggling, but your father does not put much effort into it. After all, nobody can expect a very high bride price for you, Little Comrade. Considering your mediocre looks, your lack of common sense, your shadowy history, your parents are lucky to get anything. Very soon an agreement is reached. The waiter brings beer. The adults clink their glasses and drink.

At least your father and mother are not like some parents who parade their daughter around from one town to the next, entrapping unsuspecting innocent young men and then springing a million-yuan bride price demand at the last minute.

Wang Dong murmurs. He is quiet and polite and is already calling your parents Mother and Father. With the deal done, and the beer flowing, everyone loosens up. Your father's chitchat, your mother's sighing, Wang Dong's polite behaviour – it goes as well as one can hope.

As for the wedding, the arrangements are made by your parents, who want to get it over with as quickly as possible. According to local custom, choose your wedding to coincide with a traditional holiday. Which should you choose? So many holidays, which is your favourite?

How about Lantern Festival? Not only can you see beautiful lanterns of every colour and shape, but also you can eat special tang yuan dumplings made with black sesame and other delicious fillings. Then there is Qingming Festival, where you have the pleasure of cleaning the tombstones of your ancestors. It's always important to observe this holiday – when you are deceased, you will want your children to clean your tombstone too. Naturally, this is a bad time for a wedding.

Mid-Autumn Festival is a popular, happy time, and a good time to get married. From horizon to horizon, friends exchange mooncakes in honour of the moon. But for you, since you don't really like the taste of the lotus seed filling, nor the waxy crust, nor even the newer versions of mooncakes with unusual fillings of every bizarre colour and flavour, it's not the holiday you like most. You also think it's a waste of resources, since each tiny cake comes in its own plastic container, wrapped up and boxed. But even if every year millions of these mooncakes end up in landfills, isn't it the symbolism of the festivity that counts? Besides, the waste is no worse than foreign holidays such as Halloween Night or Superbowl Day.

With so many interesting Qinese holidays, there's no need to rely on cheap cultural imports from other countries.

All those foreign holidays you were once infatuated with now sound silly, don't they? Such as Thanksgiving Day, Remembrance Day, Boxing Day and, most of all, the universally overdone Christmas Day. Possibly you are seduced by the idea of a rosy-cheeked old man in a red suit, who flies from home to home bearing gifts for children. But that is exactly the kind of idea that would weaken the minds of disciplined youth.

In any case, none of these can compare with Spring Festival, which is the most famous of all our holidays. Spring Festival, which is also Qinese New Year, is the perfect time, because all relatives are together anyway, and it's convenient to hold a wedding ceremony.

Just like that, the event is already over. The day after, your parents take you and your new husband to a small shop that sells a variety of items from children's toys to cheap luggage. Here the four of you examine suitcases and decide on a dull pink-coloured one with wheels and an extending handle.

The shopkeeper pats the hard plastic case to demonstrate its sturdiness. "This is top of the line, one hundred and fifty yuan, it'll last a long time."

Your father solemnly makes the purchase. It's your wedding gift, Little Comrade. This is the tradition, the bride's father and mother give a red suitcase, a symbol of her leaving the family. As you take the suitcase from the store, your eyes well up with sadness.

# PART FOUR

# XXXII. BEGIN MARRIED LIFE

You're married. Congratulations, Little Comrade. Now that you are a married woman, you can do no wrong. You have high social standing and social credit.

Part of the wedding deal is that Wang Dong has a house in the city, where you can live together. Now you can concentrate on treating Wang Dong like every Qinese man should be treated: Clean the home, have a son. In public give your man as much face as possible. Always be subservient and self-effacing around him. Be a doting, obedient wife. Don't worry, Little Comrade, you'll get the hang of it.

In the city, the house is not yet ready. Instead, the two of you live in the spare room of his second aunt and uncle, an unhappy couple who have made some kind of monetary arrangement with your new in-laws. It's okay, Little Comrade, everyone lies, or tells little mistruths to get what they want. Anyway, four loving relatives, all taking care of each other and enjoying each other's company in cramped quarters, that's not so bad. The only regret is that you do not have the joy of living together with your mother-in-law.

As for Dong, you don't have much to say to each other. What is there to say? In real life nobody spouts those romantic movies lines like "You are the most beautiful girl I have ever seen," or "I really like you," or "Tell me about yourself," or "I want to know all about you." That sort of silly conversation is for foreigners.

Every week your husband takes you out for an elaborate dinner at Shaxian Little Eats, the convenient fast-food noodle joint at the corner of the road. Over noodles, he plays with his phone while you play with yours.

Such a romantic dinner. Your husband holds his bowl to his mouth and scoops the rice with his chopsticks, slurping his food. He smacks his lips and spits flecks of food onto the floor. He clears phlegm from his throat and makes a puking sound into a waste bucket. He yells at the waitress when he wants some more hot water. As for you, you sit with a small bowl of ungarnished rice in front of you, nibbling from time to time. Little Comrade, don't eat too much, it's not womanly to overeat.

As you eat, silly thoughts bounce about in your empty head. An ad on your phone of a white man reminds you of Steve. Turn off your phone, like a rational and mature person, and think about having a baby boy with your husband.

As for a fast life with a foreign man like Steve, it's not for you. You don't know of any designer brand labels, you do not drink wine or enjoy expensive restaurants. So why would a big-spending foreigner interest you? None of that living has anything to do with you.

Not to be insulting, but to put it frankly, you are just like the aunties in your neighbourhood. For the most part you look like them. Except you are slim and have an A-cup bosom, whereas their bodies are more round and chesty.

"Dong. There are so many girls, why me? I'm a nobody, I don't deserve to be with such a good guy like you. You're a son, such a lucky person, you're way above me."

Hard to get those words out of your throat, but they do come.

It's a hard question to answer, Little Comrade, like so many questions that blurt out of your mouth. Fortunately, Wang Dong handles it with care.

"I had to marry someone, didn't I?"

Even though he has grease on his lips, you can go ahead and let him kiss you. Such public displays of affection are frowned upon. But in your case, Little Comrade, an exception can be made considering how sad your life is. Just a little one on the cheek.

Finally, Wang Dong leans over and kisses you. It's such a delightful surprise, isn't it? A privilege to be kissed by Wang Dong, an only son, the light and love of our collective society.

# XXXIII. MARRIAGE IS COMMITMENT

Time passes. A month, half a year, a whole year. The "honeymoon period" is over, to put it simply. By now you feel adequately depressed. Being emotional is okay. You are a woman and prone to emotional fragility. Just in time, you find a cheerful message on your phone, from your friend Apple.

> Dear Little Comrade,
> Sorry I haven't been writing lately. I've enclosed a photo of my darling boy. Isn't he so big now? He's everything I ever wanted, I'm so happy. Once you have a baby boy, you can take him to the park too.
> Your friend, Apple

What a sweet letter. You must feel such joy for your friend. You quickly tap out some unsavoury words and press enter to send the message.

Instead of your message appearing in the chat window, a notification pops up telling you your bad words have been blocked. Almost like the software is automatically scanning your messages for inappropriate language. Very useful, right?

"Nice talking to you," writes Apple. "I'm happy to hear you're doing so well. Talk to you soon!"

Why get so upset? You need to relax. In today's world, overuse of technology can cause all kinds of stress disorders. If you can't deal with it, just turn off your phone. It's easy, just hold the power button down, and count one two three.

But you do not turn off your phone. Like so many young people, you are attached to it, like a fetus is attached by umbilical cord to its parent.

Oddly enough, as happily married as you are, you are still obsessed with Steve. All night you stare at a photo of the handsome giant on your phone. Why do you keep practising that English phrase "I love you," repeating it over and over to the photo? And why do you ask that inanimate photo, "What would our child look like?" Those phrases are not useful for someone in your situation. If you want to study English, try learning Business English.

Perhaps a phrase like "The Qinese economy is strong and powerful."

So Wang Dong isn't the blond-haired, green-eyed, muscle-bound jock you wanted. Dong is a bit shorter than you, picks his nose and spits a lot. He smokes and spits pellets of food when eating, he spends all his time playing video games. These are cute character traits that will grow on you. What's most important is that he's Qinese, he's one of your tribe, just like a family member, just like your own brother or father.

Whether or not you are happy in marriage is one thing. Wang Dong's satisfaction in you is altogether another matter. Under the covers, he pokes at your scrawny, naked body.

"What's wrong?" you ask.

"The first night of our marriage, you didn't paint the bedsheets a beautiful red colour."

"I don't know what you're talking about."

Why not be truthful, Little Comrade? Marriage is all about telling the truth, revealing all your "dirty laundry" to your husband. In your heart, you know what he means. You can feel his eyes staring at you, searching for clues. Maybe you should divert his attention by saying something every man wants to hear.

"Do you want to have a baby with me? A son?" you say. "I'd like to have your son."

"Okay." He grunts his approval.

"But for a baby, we need more money. I'll get a part-time job and save up. There's a restaurant nearby I used to work at."

Good, Little Comrade. At this point who you're married to doesn't matter, so why not get on with your life? One man is as good as another, right? You may be bored with your marriage and your man. Surely, having a baby will make life more interesting.

Steve is not here, and you only have Wang Dong. So might as well have a baby with him. After all, how much time do you have left? Your female body is like a clock counting backwards. Your value is declining by the very minute. Now that you are married, do the deed while your body can handle it.

Think about it this way – a young woman who constantly switches boyfriends is bad, just like a country that constantly switches leaders is bad. That's why a one-party system without term limits is beneficial. The nation can benefit from firm and constant leadership, much like your love life.

# XXXIV. SAY HELLO
# TO OLD FRIENDS

The next day you make your way over to Su'ke, the restaurant where you used to work. Outside the shop door you look in through the window, awash with memories. That was an innocent time, right? Before you turned to prostituting your body for cash and notoriety.

Now with a second chance, hopefully, you will make better decisions. Better a waitress than pimping yourself out in a smoky karaoke bar, guzzling alcohol every night.

Inside the window, you see someone who looks familiar. A young woman about your age stands by the cash register, organizing some napkins in a pile on the counter. She wears an orange cap and has her hair pulled back in a fishnet, showing her heart-shaped face. It looks like Bo Bo, but how could it be?

It's been over a year since you talked to her. All this time you had her name in your WeChat contacts, but you always avoided messaging her. Who can blame you, Little Comrade? Every time you thought of her, you were reminded of that painful night when someone took your innocence.

But the memories are worse than reality. Seeing her in person, you feel as though a weight is lifted from your shoulders. You want to talk to her again.

You stick your head through the door. "Bo Bo?"

"Hey, Little Comrade?"

"It really is you, Bo Bo."

"Yeah. I quit the KTV after what happened. I couldn't keep working there; I sobered up. I remembered you liked working in this restaurant so much, so I asked them for a job. Now I'm living with a coworker in her flat. Wow, you look amazing, so different."

Even Bo Bo can tell, you look more beautiful than before. You see, women are more attractive if they are married and have good Qinese husbands.

"What are you doing here?" she asks. "Want a job?"

"Haha, yeah, I do."

"That's perfect. We need someone. We had a renovation, see?" You notice the interior design is different, new counters in a different spot, new tables and seats, new uniforms.

"Come with me, I'll get you started. We're doing things differently now, more professional. Hey, what's that on your finger?"

"Oh, it's my wedding ring. Yeah, I've been married for over a year."

"Really? Who's your guy?"

"Oh, someone, never mind. I should take it off. I don't want to lose it. Show me what to do. What's changed?" Okay, Little Comrade, you can take off your wedding ring. Put it in your purse for safekeeping, since you are a good caring wife.

"Oh? Haha," Bo Bo says. Bo Bo is obviously more mature now. Like you, she has gotten over her wild days. Her voice is even tempered, free of that incessant giggling noise she used to make.

"First things first. You have to sign in every day otherwise you won't get paid."

She shows you a machine attached to the wall, a fingerprint scanner. "Pretty neat, right? State-of-the-art."

Even in a small shop like Su'ke, one of countless fast-food shops around the country, advanced technology like this can be found, a sure sign that the country's economy is developing quickly.

In the back, a new mechanism, a monstrous-looking machine with a conveyor belt, washes and dries the dishes.

"What a contraption. Why not just put the plates in the sink?" you ask.

Don't be such a country bumpkin, Little Comrade. New innovations will boost the economy and move us toward higher skilled, service-oriented jobs.

"Honestly, it's very finicky," Bo Bo says. "Every other day it breaks down. Most of the time, we use the sink just as much."

Bo Bo has turned into a good leader and fine example. Luckily for you, working in the restaurant is not hard. Having worked here before, even a simpleton like you should have no trouble.

"We have a new policy for greeting customers. You know we used to say, 'Hey-Hi-Ho, so nice to see you.' Now we say, 'Wel-wel-welcome to Su-Su-Su'ke!' Make sure you use an energetic, friendly voice. Want to get started right away?"

The restaurant layout is different and the food options have doubled. Serving trays of ready-to-eat food are neatly laid out under the hot lamps, with beds of hot water flowing underneath to keep the food steamy hot. Meat and fish dishes are first in the line, then hot veggies, then finally cold stuff, like garlic spicy cucumber, duck eggs, cold rolled tofu skins, peanuts, seaweed cords, cold broccoli, cold mogu mushrooms and black fungus petals.

Having familiarized yourself with your new workplace, you begin your shift. The evening passes without any problem. Your feet hurt and your hands are sore, but the pain only brings back fond memories.

As the night progresses, the entrance door opens and a big, blond-haired, foreign man enters. Your eyes zero in on his face and your heart beats fast.

"Steve?" you mumble. Yes, it is he, Once-upon-a-time-in-KFC Steve.

Of course, you have no interest in him now that you are a happily married woman. But while Steve eats dinner, you stare over in his direction. Perhaps you are just trying to be an attentive waitress?

"I can't believe it, it's Steve," you whisper to Bo Bo when you sneak over to her side.

"Yeah. He comes a lot. He tutors a wealthy student who lives in the nice apartment complex across the street. I was going to tell you."

"Does he still teach at the English centre?"

"Yeah, he does. I even enrolled in his class. It's a bit far for me to go there, but he got me a good deal. After he's finished his meal, I'll introduce you to him."

As excited as you are, try to take a breath. What's all the fuss about? Perhaps it's because you want to study English and improve yourself. It's undeniable that English is an essential skill in today's global economy. That's why English is a mandatory class for students across the country. No shame in trying to improve the level of your English.

Too bad you don't have a ring on your finger otherwise Steve could see you are married. Are you sure you don't want to put it on so that he knows?

Near his table, you repeatedly wipe clean a chair. You cannot gather the courage to look him in the face, so you cannot tell whether his eyes are looking at you, studying your features, appreciating your beauty.

Is it the delicious aroma of the food that is causing you to salivate? Your fingers pull at the fabric covering your groin, like you are in heat. Perhaps you need to use the bathroom? Luckily you are not like those mobs of schoolgirls who cannot control themselves at the sight of a handsome foreigner.

"This is my friend, Little Comrade," Bo Bo says, coming to your side.

"Oh, hi, hello to both of you." Steve grabs your hand. His grip is so strong and manly. Why do you feel so dizzy?

Conversation flows by. You mumble, dazed. When you come to, you see that Steve is gone. Slowly you clean his plates and food tray. What is that afterglow on your face? Perhaps you've been inspired to learn English. After work Bo Bo pats you on the back.

"So should we go?" she asks.

"Go where?"

"Don't you remember? Steve invited you to take some free classes. He said he would enroll you, no charge, for night classes."

So smitten were you by the musicality of the new language that you must have lost track of what Steve said. Don't be tricked by Steve's offer. The evening classes are offered free of charge to the community at large. They're simply a marketing gimmick.

"Oh yeah, haha. For sure, let's go!"

"Studying English is useful even if we have jobs like this. I don't plan on working in the restaurant forever. When my English is good enough I'm going to work for a foreign company. Anyway, Steve is a great teacher."

Now that you have a husband, Little Comrade, you can turn your efforts to helping society.

# XXXV. NEVER GIVE UP ON SELF-IMPROVEMENT

That is why you go to the English centre. To increase your skills, to become a productive citizen.

The English centre where Steve works is the same as before, located on a quiet road lined with trees, shops and residential compounds. From the street, it has a modest appearance, no more than a window and door. On one side is a grilled chicken stall that cooks takeout, handing paper bags to Meituan delivery boys at all hours of the day and night.

Upstairs, in a classroom, you see the giant.

"Hi, Teacher Steve," Bo Bo chirps. "How you today? Remember my friend I tell you about, Little Comrade?" Her English is unexpectedly good, right? She has improved through studious effort.

"Oh yeah." Steve pats you on the back and ushers you into a chair. "Welcome to my class, ha ha! Get ready to be wowed."

You allow yourself to slide into the bucket chair. Obviously, it is not Steve's handsome looks that cause you to be so malleable. Most likely it is the torrent of strange sounds, the English words and characters that bombard you from the whiteboard. Take a deep breath, Little Comrade, you will persevere. Learning English will show foreigners that Qinese can speak any language elegantly and without accent.

"So, you admit he's handsome, right?" you whisper to Bo Bo.

"He's not bad. There was a younger, muscular guy before, you would have liked that one. I don't really find Steve attractive. Doesn't the smell of alcohol from his breath bother you?"

"I don't notice anything."

What exactly are you discussing, Little Comrade? Since you are married, obviously you cannot discuss the good looks of any man other than your husband, except perhaps a few of our country's handsome movie stars. Anyway, everyone knows that foreigners smell, it's their body odour, a foul smell. Why else do they always smear their armpits with wax and butter?

Somehow you manage to wiggle your way onto the school roster, paying only a nominal fee. All the romantic experience you had is paying off. You flash a couple of well-timed smiles and bat your eyelashes. The dumb foreigner writes your name down on the student name sheet. Good thinking, Little Comrade, you have managed to outsmart this foreigner.

Very quickly you get into the habit of studying English. To your credit, you do spend a large amount of time studying the actual subject matter carefully with your eyes, and, when the opportunity presents itself, with your mouth.

The rest of the time, you shop for school supplies. You buy little bags for your pens and then bags for your pen bags. You buy corrective tape and fluid, pencils and erasers. You spend every free moment in the school, often sitting in the cramped hall where students eat their home-cooked lunches.

At home – in Wang Dong's aunt and uncle's cramped apartment – you lie with Wang Dong after he has used your body to satisfy his primitive urges. It's a romantic time, which he usually passes by smoking a cigarette and playing on his phone. However, tonight he wants to talk.

"Where have you been going so often? To see your friend Bo Bo?"

"I'm taking English classes. I thought I told you."

"What? Why?"

"I already paid for the tuition, it's not refundable. I have my weekly review coming up, I can't miss it. Anyway, I'm a married woman now, what do you have to worry about?"

Yes, it's true, now that you are married it will be easy for you to ignore all the foreigners. After all, a wife has a high social credit trustworthiness score.

It is in the nation's interest for you to continue your studies. Elevate your learning, become a master of English. Just be sure to be honest with your husband and with yourself.

After Dong goes to shower, why do you snicker? Are you hiding something? What has gotten into you?

The night of your weekly review comes. In the classroom, it's just you and Steve, alone.

"So, how are you finding the classes?" he asks.

"I having lot of fun. I want improve even more. Maybe I can get a good job, better job." That's wonderful, Little Comrade.

The little room you are in, with the door closed, is quiet and intimate. Steve sits across from you, so close you can almost feel his breath, smell his husky odour. Doesn't that make you want to sit farther away? Why do you lean forward, as if you want to smell him more?

Steve's face is handsome. As a married woman, you can admit it without being tempted to give into desire. A blond, male teacher with a square jaw, big beautiful eyes. But really, your husband has eyes just like those, although they are beadier, smaller, darker. Steve has some slight stubble on his face and big manly hands.

"So nice to see you every week," Steve says. "I hope you'll come over for a private lesson, it's free for you." He winks.

What is this conniving foreigner up to? Is he trying to suggest that you go over to his house for free English lessons? If so, perhaps you should take him up on that offer. After all there's no need to feel bad about taking advantage of foreigners. Their generosity is usually just a cover for some scheme to exploit citizens of poor nations. He probably doesn't realize that you are married and he has no chance with you.

"Yes, I'd love to come over," you say. Watch your feet, Little Comrade. Your feet are sticking too far under the table and are in contact with Steve's feet. It's unhygienic and can spread germs. If you really need to stretch out your legs at least take off your shoes.

With your shoes off, you touch Steve's leg. Both of you are squirming in your chairs. How uncomfortable he must feel. Except he is smiling for some bizarre reason. These foreign men are inexplicable.

Even if you are sexually aroused, it is impossible to act on your desires, given that you are happily married to a Qinese man. Anyway, someone like Steve, who cannot even do such a simple thing as order a chicken fried rice from the shop across the street, cannot possibly compete with your husband.

"So, when are you coming to my place for extra lessons?" He smiles and winks. The winking means he has something in his eye, right? Perhaps you should offer him a tissue. Other women might flirt with him, they might cheapen our whole nation. This kind of lack of critical thinking, combined with a wild imagination, is particularly dangerous. Luckily you are much smarter than that.

# XXXVI. SERVE IN THE NAME OF OUR COUNTRY

Over the next week, you work in Su'ke during the day, study in the evening and take care of your husband at night. When you have free time, you go out with your best friend, Bo Bo.

"How's married life?" Bo Bo asks. "Is it as bad as you thought it would be?"

You giggle. "No, I was totally wrong, it's fun." Good, Little Comrade, be a good role model for your friend.

Work hard; mind your own business; have a normal, decent, ordinary life with a good Qinese husband. If you have a chance, study to increase your economic contribution to society.

Downtown, on fashion street, you walk with your friend, drinking bubble tea. Two pretty young women arm in arm. At the end of this street is a park. Supposedly it is the nicest park in the city, but there is an admission fee, and you have never been inside it.

On both sides of this street are storefronts. A big traditional-looking building in the Ming period stands over everything. It is a famed noodle shop that serves traditional-style noodles in a special sauce.

This commercial area is known for many upper end clothing boutiques. But the shops have dwindled in number. Everywhere you look are shuttered windows. Customers no longer visit these shops. Instead, people buy online, using sites like Tmall, JD and Taobao.

You pass by a shop that is going out of business. There is a discounted dress in the store's window display.

"Do you think Teacher Steve would like that?"

"Yeah, maybe." Bo Bo giggles. "Why?"

"He asked me over to his apartment," you say, hands clasped to your small chest.

"You're not pulling my leg? He really invited you over? Are you sure he means it in that way?"

What is "that" way, Little Comrade? Something neither of you wants to say out loud. But you both know what it is. Why not say it out loud, so that others can hear?

Foreign English teachers in our country, who are mostly male, are known to frequent the homes of their young female students and vice versa. So perhaps it's not out of the ordinary; nothing more than regular English learning will transpire.

At night, you toss and turn in bed, and hide under the covers, playing with your phone.

What are you looking up? All those search terms, like "How to get a foreign man to like you," and "What dating a foreign man is like," and "What babies look like with a foreign man," these embarrassing searches, even though users may delete them from their phone's browser history, are still kept in government records.

At home, the next day, you pick out some clothes. Your wardrobe contains the proper clothes of a married woman, very modest. In order to take advantage of Steve, you need to dress like a prostitute, right? You pick out something and use a pair of scissors to cut a few holes in it.

As for shoes, foreign guys like this Steve expect womanly high heels. You take out your best, a pair of silver strap high heels. They hurt your feet, but they look appropriate for your costume.

In your tight clothes, your A-cup looks like a stuffed D-cup. Pretending to have a large bosom doesn't bother you. Obviously, Steve would never see you naked, because only your Qinese husband can see that, right? Also, you put on heavy makeup and slap your lips to make them puffy, because you have heard foreign men like puffy mouths.

Wang Dong sits on the bed, playing his chicken dinner game. "I have an English lesson, I'll be back later tonight," you say, giggling and slamming the door behind you. Little Comrade, be careful, such force could damage the hinges.

Having manoeuvred yourself into a position where you can exploit this foreigner for free lessons, you meet Steve by the river.

Under the sun, you catch Steve gawking at you in your most revealing outfit, short shorts with black-and-white stripes, short sleeve shirt with a picture of cat.

"To be honest, you are so hot," Steve says.

"Oh yeah?" you say. "I think you so handsome too."

Little Comrade, use his vanity against him. You'll be able to take advantage of his ego to get free lessons. Perhaps Steve has other ideas in his head, not just teaching you grammar rules and spelling. He puts his arm around you.

"Can I kiss you?" he says.

"Okay."

Just like that, he kisses you on the cheek. Well done, Little Comrade, this foreigner has kissed a married Qinese woman. Again you've shown that he is unworthy of being in our country, that he's a snake and a villain.

Now to spring the final trap on him. Before he can protest, you force your lips onto his. See his reaction. See if he has any morals. If he has any value as a decent human being, he will object. He will recoil and push you away. But, obviously, being the slimeball that he is, he does not.

The warmth of his breath makes your body tingle. You feel a sudden uncontrollable urge to take off your clothes. Finally, a foreigner who desires you. Right, Little Comrade? But now you are married and mature enough to reject him.

"No, you not Qinese. And I have confession, I have Qinese husband."

"Oh yeah?" he says. "That makes it even more exciting."

"Yeah, too bad, right?" You giggle.

Obviously, nothing more can occur between the two of you, since you are a married Qinese woman. Tell him again about your husband. That should scare him into leaving you alone.

"You know," he says, "even if you have a husband, if you're not happy, it doesn't count."

"Take me go your home and pa-pa-pa, okay?" you say, holding on to his sleeve. Now is the time to entwine him in a web of trouble. You're overcome with a desire to convict him of a crime, right? Otherwise, why would you not uphold your virtue? Why else would you give in and spread your legs for this not particularly handsome international playboy?

"Sure," he says, taking you by the hand. Little Comrade, you are certainly a good actor, trying to get evidence of his wrongdoing.

At his home, the two of you experience intimacy. Bugs chirp outside. The pain and discomfort, the shame you feel from sleeping and soiling your Qinese body with an uncouth foreign man must be horrible. But, for the sake of proving this foreign man is evil, it's worth it. Do what you have to do to implicate the foreigner.

Having triggered Steve's lust, he forces himself on you, committing atrocities against your body. Such sickening acts, unthinkable, like kissing with the lights on. That must make you want to kill yourself, right? Hang in there, Little Comrade. His terrible actions cause you to lose yourself. You scream and groan uncontrollably. Finally, you have gotten the evidence you need to convict this foreigner of seducing a married woman.

How much it must hurt, Steve smacking you in bed like that, over and over, until you are yelling and sobbing so loudly your voice is hoarse. Over and over, he pounds you, it must be humiliating. How much you have sacrificed for your country. Your screaming is so frightening that you try to stop yourself by covering your mouth with his, clutching him so tightly, your fingernails draw his blood. No need to do that.

Next day, at school, you look for Steve. But he is nowhere to be seen.

"Where's Steve?" you ask the secretary.

"Didn't you hear? His visa got revoked."

"No, how come?"

The secretary shrugs. "It happens sometimes. Everyone knows he was doing bad things with female students. It's illegal, so the police asked him to leave. He wasn't very happy about it."

Well, Little Comrade, what did you expect?

# XXXVII. LEARN TO RESOLVE LOVERS' ARGUMENTS

Over the next few days, you wallow in pitiful thoughts. It doesn't matter where you are, at home or outside.

So sad. All day and night you think of your former teacher. Don't fret, your English skills are already good enough. You have used this foreign man to your full advantage and there is no point of continuing the relationship. Still, oddly enough, the cloud of unhappiness floats around your head.

You exhibit other, unusual behaviour. For example, every time you pass by a closed-circuit camera, you raise your middle finger to it. "Hey, fuck you," you shout, facing the camera lens. What obscene, preposterous language.

Who are you speaking to, Little Comrade? You have been doing that a lot lately, why? Stop looking into the cameras, stop covering your face every time you pass one by.

Even in your misery, a normal day comes and goes. Wang Dong goes out to do what he likes, and you tag along like a good wife.

In the afternoon you find yourself with Dong in a sleazy, smoky, government approved and licensed web bar. He wants to try a new computer game, but he doesn't bother explaining that to you.

Although Wang Dong is perfect for you in every way, sometimes you feel he ignores you, or treats you like a child.

At the registration counter, Wang Dong produces his identity card. The cashier, a good-looking young girl, doesn't ask if you want a computer too.

It's so smoky, you cough. Everyone in the web café smokes, it burns your eyes. Sitting beside Wang Dong, you see his avatar running around on the computer screen, shooting and killing. It may not be something exciting to you, but at least your husband is having fun.

"This is the newest chicken dinner game," Wang Dong says. "I'm going to win a chicken dinner for sure."

Perhaps this is not the life you wanted, sitting in a smoky web café beside your husband, watching him play video games. Maybe you saw yourself with a handsome foreign man, living a high-class life, going to the English opera house, listening to a live band, drinking red and white wines. But this is reality. Isn't this life good enough for you? It's good enough for your classmates, your peers, your friends, why not you?

All the patrons of the web café look a bit unnatural, maybe because of the glowing computer monitors, the low ceiling, the smoky air, the rapt and mesmerized expressions of the video gamers. You are the only one standing there looking around as if you are in an eerie wasteland.

After a few hours, Wang Dong is in a foul mood, having failed to win a chicken dinner. What's more, the whole day you have been a bad, inattentive wife. Soon you are back home, lying in bed with him. Even though you had a busy and exciting day, you are still depressed about losing your free English teacher.

Despite having attained a satisfactory level of English, you still want to improve. But there's something else on your mind. You're not imagining, for instance, travelling abroad with Steve, are you? Like so many ideas that inexplicably pop into your head, you notice an impulsive longing to expand your education with Steve, to travel with him and leave the country of your birth, to see the wider world.

Fortunately, your husband is by your side. His closeness gives you a feeling of safety.

"I want to go on a vacation," you say.

"No money."

"Just a short trip."

"Where?"

"North America."

Wang Dong jerks his head back and frowns. He doesn't need to say it out loud, Little Comrade, but you don't have money to go anywhere, especially not to North America.

And even if you did, why choose such a faraway place? Why not Taiwan? Or Thailand? Vietnam is also a popular destination; you can take a cruise from Hong Kong. There's lots of seafood. When you post photos to your friends, they'll gossip at how much money you have. If you really must be a show-off, pick the Maldives.

But why travel at all? The best sights are in Qina, your home country. You can see the Great Wall of Qina, terracotta warriors, the Forbidden City, the Summer Palace, even go to Tibet if you are feeling adventurous. What can those newfangled countries so far away offer in terms of sightseeing? As for the Eiffel Tower, or other unremarkable foreign landmarks, you can view all of those conveniently in one day, at one of the many "miniature world" theme parks in our country.

What's more, all kinds of dangers lurk abroad, and you can be subjected to violence at a whim. So many angry, unhappy people ready to bash you over the head with a club for the simple reason that your eyes and skin look different from theirs.

In your own country, you have all the delicious food you want, as well as being surrounded by people who behave just like you, and don't take you to task for your ordinary behaviour.

"You're impossible," Wang Dong says. "What kind of wife wants to travel, see the world? Stay at home, be respectable, have a family instead."

"I don't want to stay at home. I don't want to have a family with you."

Dong slaps you on the face. Don't worry, it's just a small, harmless slap. The pain will go away. Take a deep breath.

Don't be alarmed by the physical nature of your interaction. This sort of domestic altercation is expected, and a sign of a developing relationship. It's the natural tension between husband and wife, lover and beloved. Good marriages come with growing pains.

"Don't you think I know what you've been doing?" Wang Dong says. "Always going off, spending time with that English teacher. You're a terrible wife, a disgrace to me. Get out."

"Why should I go?"

"Leave, this isn't even your home."

"Are you or aren't you my husband?"

"Who knows! Everyone can see you're not the wife-type at all. Your parents ripped me off, your family members are all scammers. It's obvious you weren't a fresh girl and mutai-solo when we got married. A man knows such things. Tell me, did you ever sleep with anyone before we married?"

"I'm not leaving."

"See, you can't answer me."

"I was fresh, I was!"

"You're lying. Go away, go for a walk, before I throw you out."

You let yourself out of the bedroom. In the living room, you look around. Remember to put your coat on before you go out, Little Comrade. After you have your coat on, you can go out. The metal door creaks when you open it. The concrete stairwell goes down a few flights of stairs to the ground floor and the courtyard of the complex.

After moping for a while, kicking dirt and rocks around the block, you go back up the flight of stairs. You try your key, but the door is bolted from the inside.

"Auntie?" You knock. "Let me in."

"Go away."

"Where's Wang Dong?"

"He doesn't want to see you. You're an immoral, shameless woman. Go find someplace else to live."

"I don't have anywhere else."

"That's your problem."

"I have no money, just let me get my things."

"It's all in a pile, under the staircase at the bottom of the building."

"Please, let me in."

"Go away. You can call him in a week and see what he says. Now get lost, before I call the police."

Don't be naive, Little Comrade, with your impulsive comings and goings, everyone suspects you of something naughty. Wang Dong is not stupid – all Qinese men know when they are being made to wear a "green hat." They also know if their woman has lied to them about being a virgin.

Behind the residential complex is a rectangular man-made pond. The pond looks more like a bottomless sewage reservoir, holding black water. A few fountains spray liquid from the oily surface. Flanking this place are a few residential communities, with a guard sleeping at the entrance.

By the pond, you stare out over the water. Look down, Little Comrade, what do you see? It's your own face, framed by bangs of black hair, unwashed, and baggy eyes. You look sad and tired, what's happened to you? So old already. Your unsatisfactory appearance may be a result of overexertion. Too much physical merrymaking.

Lover and husband both gone, so fitting, Little Comrade. Now there's nowhere for you to go, except to find Bo Bo and stay with her for a while.

The memory of losing Steve makes visiting the English centre unbearable, so you avoid it.

Luckily Bo Bo lives only a short DiDi car ride away. When Bo Bo opens her door and sees you with your two big bags of belongings, she knows what has happened.

"What am I going to do?" you sob into her shoulder.

"I don't know. Have a rest, drink some tea." She sits you down on the hardwood sofa and boils some tea.

"Steve's gone. I'll never see him again."

"So it's Steve you miss, not your husband?"

"I don't know."

"Maybe you can find a way to see him again. Write him a letter. Tell him how you feel. Maybe he'll come back."

"It's hopeless."

"Hey. Remember that Qinese-American teacher we met once? Mark, that's his name. We sat in on his class a long time ago, the first time we went to the English centre. Remember the way he looked at you? Anyway, he travels a lot, back and forth to America, I heard classmates talking about it. Maybe there's a way Mark can help you get to America, and you can be with Steve again," Bo Bo says.

"Yeah? You really think Mark would help me?"

"Maybe, who knows. Anyway, have a rest. Come on, you can sleep in my bed with me. Just like old times."

# PART
# FIVE

# XXXVIII. FIND NEW OPPORTUNITIES

Not that night, but a following night that week, Bo Bo's words begin to have an effect on you. What she says ignites your imagination. The delayed result is explosive, like firecrackers at the end of a long fuse.

You don't know precisely how you find your way over to the English centre, with its blue shopfront. But there you are, outside on the sidewalk, unable to decide what to do. Too nervous to go in yet unwilling to leave.

Students begin coming down the stairs, exiting to the street where you are. It is late already. The last class has just let out. Not having the fortitude to go inside to look for the "American" teacher named Mark, you duck into a side street where some public bicycles are locked in a row waiting to be used.

A few students walk by. You tilt your head down and fiddle with the nearest bicycle, trying to pass off as an ordinary worker going home. Have all the students and teachers left the centre? Is it safe to raise your head now? You might as well give up, no one is left. The streets are all dark and quiet.

Just as you are getting bored with your playacting, you hear someone beside you. A small object falls accidentally near your foot. Look down, what do you see? It is a public transport card, which can be used for transit buses as well as the public bicycles that are so conveniently placed all around the city.

"Buhaoyisi," says a voice. The word is spoken in Qinese, but something is not quite right with the accent. You have heard a similar "buhaoyisi" before. It sounds like a foreigner. You jerk your head up expecting to see Steve, your long-lost teacher.

But no, it is not Steve. It is a Qinese face, a teacher that you seem to recognize – Mark. The streetlight is casting its yellow glow off to the side. Even in the shadows you recognize him.

"Is this yours?" You bend down and pick up the transit card.

"Thanks," says Mark. "You look familiar, are you a student?"

"Yeah, I was. I was Steve's student. I miss him."

"Oh yeah? Too bad he went back to his home country. He was a good teacher."

"Yeah. Hey, you can speak Putonghua." You didn't know what to expect, if he was in fact pretending to be a foreigner or not. His Putonghua, although it carries a strange accent, is passable, even fluent.

"Yeah," says Mark.

"I saw you teaching in the English centre once. They said you're a foreign teacher."

"Oh yeah, I think I remember. That was a while ago. You came in once, into my class, and sat in the back with a friend. Am I right?"

"You have a good memory."

"And you're very pretty," he says. "That's probably why I remember you so well."

It's hard not to be flattered by this smooth-talking, globe-trotting person. You're beginning to think of him as a real foreigner, despite his Qinese face.

Before speaking to him, this Mark was, in your view, a fraudster, someone you avoided at all costs. But after just a few words with him, you begin to think he is a human being like you.

"Are you going home now?" you ask.

"Well, I was. But, hey, I'm a bit hungry. Want to join me for a quick bite to eat?"

"Yeah, sure, why not?"

There's a tiny halal Lanzhou hand-pulled noodle restaurant that's always open past midnight right on this road, on the opposite side of the small street where you are standing.

Three small heavy tables with marble centres and wood frames, each big enough for two people, are inside the shop. A small kitchen in the back is separated by a floating wall.

Mark is sitting in front of you, telling you about himself. In the light of the restaurant, up close, he seems less threatening than when you first came across him in the classroom.

Perhaps it's because the first time you saw him, he was an unexpected, even unwelcomed, sight. A Qinese face when you expected to see a foreign face. A Qinese doppelgänger for your all-American Steve.

Now that you have gotten over your surprise and initial disappointment, your mind is opening up to new possibilities. Or perhaps it is because he is speaking Qinese, your language. You can understand his jokes, his charming, even cute, way of speaking. He makes a mistake, an accidental, awkward pun, and you laugh. His handle on the language is not perfect. But it is far from inadequate. He seems to know enough to make you fall in love with him at least.

Not that it is a big deal, but have you noticed, Little Comrade, that you fall in love too quickly? But, never mind, that is a topic for another day.

"So, you really are from America?" you say. "I didn't believe it at first. Sorry, I don't mean to be rude – I was just surprised."

"That's okay. Actually, if you want to know the truth, I don't like telling people I'm from America."

"No? Why not? America is a great country, isn't it? Everyone wants to go there."

"All countries are more or less the same. Anyway, I'm Qinese, too. I just used my American citizenship to help me get a teaching job here. I'm no different than you are, really. I can speak Qinese fluently, can't I?"

"That's true," you say. "Your Qinese is very good. You must have had much practice with many girlfriends, am I right? Maybe you're able to hone your skill at home with your wife, no?"

"I'm not married," he says. "How about you?"

You shake your head in reply. "I have no man at home, if that's what you're asking." Mark turns and asks the waiter, a fourteen-year-old boy with a budding black moustache, the son of the proprietors, for some tea.

While you have the chance, you look at Mark more closely. He isn't half bad looking. In fact, he has quite a good body. He's slim, not overly muscular. He has rather large eyes, with double eyelids, something that you like. Compared to Wang Dong, Mark is a handsome devil. Oh, when will you learn, Little Comrade?

The watery, thin, lukewarm tea comes. The boy waiter leaves the flimsy, tin pot on your table before retiring to an adjacent table to play a game on his phone. The shop master, the waiter's father, is a short, powerfully built man, wearing a taqiyah, a Muslim cap. He stands at the open entrance, hands on his hips, looking out into the night. But you miss all of these details, since Mark has captivated your attention.

"So, what do you do?" he asks you. "It's nearly ten o'clock at night. Shouldn't you be at home sleeping? Or are you one of those party girls?"

"I'm not one of those party girls, quite the opposite in fact. Actually, I used to work at a computer factory, but I quit. Now I'm just hanging out, taking a break for a while, looking for a job."

The food is eaten, the bill is paid. But the conversation continues outside as you walk with him. The stroll is a romantic one, and it passes almost like in a movie. You listen to his deep, charming voice with its curious accent and phrasing, about his life, his parents, his sisters and cousins, and about the life of the Qinese living overseas. He tells you that it's not all that different from life here, in Qina. And yet, when he describes it, you are enchanted and want to know more and more.

"Are there really that many Qinese people overseas?" you ask.

"Sure, there are," he says. "It's quite normal. There's a big world out there. Haven't you ever thought of going abroad too?"

"Yes. I mean, I'd love to. If I could, one day." There's something about the idea that makes you almost stutter. It's like trying to give voice to your deepest secret desire, which you are afraid of confessing.

During this time, the two of you have been walking away from the English centre. You cross a small bridge over a tiny river, and then walk through a park along the bank. You are near the building where Mark lives.

"Want to come up for a moment, just to sit?" he says.

Haven't you been in a situation like this before? You know the answer should be "No, thanks." Still, somehow you find yourself hesitating. You want to accept the invitation.

"Okay, maybe just for a minute."

Since you are a divorced woman, spurned by society, you can let any man do what he wants to you.

Perhaps this is all for the best. After all, Mark is no ordinary person. Firstly, he's American, isn't he? How many Americans do you know? None, other than Mark, and you probably won't have the chance to meet another. In fact, there's a good chance he's the only one in the whole city. Secondly, now that you've talked to him for what seems like hours, his charming attitude makes you feel safe. Thirdly, he tells you he lives in a nice, serviced apartment. You want to see this nice place.

Then, somewhat embarrassingly, there is a new feeling you have, which is harder to pin down. It's the subconscious feeling that you want to be with another man in order to erase the previous failures, the previous disgusting acts that you committed with Q, with Dong and with Steve. Oh, Little Comrade, as if adding more disgusting acts to your resumé could dilute and lessen the intensity and authenticity of each.

In any case, however strong or weak your arguments are, there you are with him in the elevator. Upstairs, the hallway is wide, tastefully decorated with white panels that feature a bevelled bamboo flower design. The doors to each room are spaced apart generously. Above each door is a high-energy, focused light, which turns on by sound. Along the corridor's ceiling are more lights, the bulbs hidden from view by overlapping surfaces.

Inside Mark's studio room it's breathtaking. It looks like a five-star hotel. However, Little Comrade, you don't know that, since you have never seen what a room in a five-star hotel looks like.

All the furniture is equally tasteful and perfect. In the kitchenette is a full-sized brand name fridge. Also present is a brand new laundry machine with dryer function, a rare and remarkable item. There is a microwave and two sinks – one in the kitchenette and one in the bathroom. Even the shower stall is uniquely designed in a 360-degree shape with floor-to-ceiling glass wall, looking into the studio room. As well, the bathroom mirror has a circle of frosted glass built into it that gives off the most pleasing glow. Soft, caressing lights are tucked into every possible crevice. Even the bed's large varnished headboard has an elegant horizontal light hidden in it.

Standing at the window, you look across the entire city, all drab and dreary by comparison. You sit down on a firm, high-backed loveseat and take in your comfortable surroundings. When Mark looks at you, he finds you smiling back at him.

# XXXIX. DON'T BACK DOWN

And so begins what is a fairy-tale story for you. Each night, after he gets off work, you meet Mark and walk home with him.

Mark has a lot of free time to spend with you. When you ask him why he is so relaxed, he says it's just the life he has. He is an expat, a foreign English teacher. He shows you his passport, his working visa. All his paperwork is in order. He has a good, easy life, and you are lucky enough to be able to share it with him.

There is a saying in America, "It's too good to be true." Perhaps if you weren't so pleased with yourself and busy enjoying life while others work hard and fulfill duties to both parents and society, you would know if this saying applies to you or not.

"You know," says Bo Bo. "You've been spending a lot of time with this guy. Are you sure he is what he says he is?"

"This guy? You mean my boyfriend," you say, rather irritated by your best friend's attitude. "I don't know what your problem is. You were salty about Steve, now you're salty about Mark."

"I'm not, I just think something's strange."

"What's strange? You're the one who told me to get with Mark in the first place. Now that I'm happy, it's suddenly a problem for you?"

"Yeah, well, you should take things slow. Look what happened last time."

"What do you know? I bet you thought I had no chance to get with Mark. Now that he likes me, you're jealous, right? You thought Mark wouldn't want someone like me, and you could get a good laugh at my expense again. If so, you must be very disappointed. No wonder you're a sour grape now."

"That's not it at all. I'm just trying to look out for you. Can't you see that? You've only known Mark a short time and already he's saying he'll bring you to America. That's such a lame line right there, I'm sure he uses it on every girl he sees."

"So what?" you say. "He's a lonely guy, he's misunderstood. You haven't met him and talked to him like I have. He means it for me. Anyway, he doesn't have other girlfriends, just me. Maybe he said it to another girl before, but she's not here, is she? So I must be the lucky one. Anyway, I want to go to America, who knows, maybe I'll find Steve."

"Oh, forget about Steve. If Mark loves you, why don't you two get married? Why take you to America just on a travel visa? If you marry, you can get a green card, isn't that what they give you? Then you're a citizen. But he won't, will he? What's he hiding?"

"Isn't it enough that I can go? That he'll help me?"

"There's something fishy going on. Trust me, I know about these things. I have more street smarts than you. What are the odds he'd pick you, of all people? Of all the girls he could get, why you? Don't you think it's strange?"

"Because I'm such a nobody, right? Because I'm such a worthless person, is that what you're saying?"

"That's not what I'm saying at all."

"I can't believe you. You're so petty, you can't stand that I really am doing better than you. You lost your love. You lost your boyfriend. Nobody loves you because you sold yourself and you're a whore. But I've got someone who loves me. It must hurt you, right? Boo hoo, poor you."

"You bitch," Bo Bo says. "Get lost. Go live with your Qinese American boyfriend and die." She storms out of the room.

For a moment it stings your heart. You regret saying what you did, bringing up her ex-boyfriend. But you don't chase after her.

"She's the one that owes me an apology," you say to yourself.

When you message Bo Bo on WeChat, you find that the message does not go through. A circle with an arrow pops up. It says that the message has been successfully sent but rejected by the user. You have been blacklisted. But all you do is yawn.

# XL. ENJOY CONSENSUAL RELATIONSHIPS

It's hard to think about Bo Bo when you are lying in bed in a nice hotel suite, head burrowed in the cranny of your Qinese American boyfriend's neck, his arms around you. You have other things to think about, like what you should pack for your trip with Mark to "America."

"Mark," you say, "I'm really glad we're going to America. But have you thought about, you know, getting married? I know maybe in your culture it's too early to talk about. But, still, what do you think? I mean, you want me to come to America because you think we're going to get married eventually, right? Otherwise, what's the point of us going?"

"Of course," he says. "Let's just go first and take a look. What if you don't like it there?"

"But I have no money; it'll be expensive."

"Don't worry about that, I can pay for it. You can pay me back later when you get a job there. I'll ask my sisters to arrange something for you, what do you think?"

"Really? Oh yes, that'd be great. But doing what?"

"Don't worry, I'll take care of everything. It's much easier to make money there than it is here. You know what I mean, right? What we need to do first is get these visa application forms to the embassy."

You are so overwhelmed with happiness that you can hardly contain it. When Mark touches you, caresses you, you not only allow it to happen, you even reciprocate, touching him in return. In that gorgeous studio room, overlooking the lights of the city, a whole new world of intimacy, of romance, opens up before your eyes.

Although he has American citizenship, as he claims, he is still Qinese, with a Qinese face. And so in bed you discover that Mark, like all Qinese men, is an exceptionally good lover.

Before, you were scared. Relations between man and woman had only ever brought you pain. You never knew it could be satisfying. But Mark has demonstrated something incredible to you, something almost defying possibility. You realize a physical encounter between man and woman can be exciting, even pleasurable.

With Mark's numerable talents at your disposal, the previous injuries you suffered are washed away. Q's insults, the drunken groping inflicted by strangers, it's all forgotten and forgiven. Even Steve, your old English teacher, who you've almost forgotten, never treated you this well. And your ex, Wang Dong, who kicked you out of your home once upon a time, is nothing more than a blurry memory.

Your body contorts and spasms. Part of it is because of the pleasure, but also part of it is because of your desire to please your boyfriend, and to show him that you care for him.

Yes, he is making love to you, performing a ritual so ancient that it dates back to the legendary Yellow Emperor and even further.

Lucky for you, you know what sounds to make. Those same sounds you heard at La Viva so long ago, during the night, when you were lying awake while Q was snoring.

When the noises escape your throat, instead of sounding like you are being pleasured, it sounds like you are in pain. The crying and panic increases with the beating of your heart. It excites Mark into a flurry of desire and domination over your weaker body. In your delirium your words slur together. You babble nonsense as you gasp in the throes of ecstasy. All your embarrassment, your thoughts of your parents, of Bo Bo, of Q, of Dong, of Steve, of all your previous misfortunes, as if at the snap of a finger, are obliterated by this outpouring of bottled-up emotion.

# XLI. TAKE A BIG TRIP
# IF YOU CAN

Without ever doubting it would come to pass, you find yourself a few months later in the international airport in Shanghai.

Mark has proven himself not only capable in bed but has managed to process all the necessary paperwork for you to go with him abroad. He is sponsoring you on a tourist visa, that much he has told you. It is all a complicated mystery that goes over your head. But you are not concerned with the nitty-gritty details, only with being present when the day comes.

And sure enough, the day has come. It feels totally different from what you imagined. All your excitement about going abroad for the very first time to see a country that all of your peers, relatives, elders can only dream of seeing slips away to be replaced by nervous dread.

As you pass through the gate you look out the enormous terminal windows and see an airplane. What's the symbol on the tail of the wing? It is a red circle, with a red maple leaf in it.

This airline is called Air America, and in cooperation with our safe and financially solvent Air Qina, it runs a route between New York and Shanghai, both world-class, successful metropolises.

You have seen airplanes in movies. You've seen airplanes flying through the sky way up overhead. But this is the very first time you have seen one so up close. This is the first time you step onto an airplane and into the cabin. The air stewardess directs you down the aisle to your seat. Mark is behind you, urging you to go faster. He has been thoughtful enough to book you a window seat.

Take a look at the flight attendants. Already you see many foreign faces. A tall blond stewardess, wearing a crisply tailored vest, is speaking to passengers, helping put luggage away and in general making herself indispensable. In the other aisle, a round-bodied, pale-faced brunette stewardess beams with a smile for everyone.

In each aisle a stewardess stands, going through bizarre motions. A video plays on the monitor embedded in the seat in front of you. Unfortunately, you cannot understand the spoken English.

A moment later, however, a friendly voice comes on. The sounds you hear are your familiar Qinese. It is so comforting to your ears. It's a safety video that they are showing. Pay attention. What if the plane has an accident? You need to know what to do.

"Will the plane crash?" you ask Mark.

"No, it won't. Planes only crash because of terrorists. Do you see any terrorists here?"

You crane your head around. Do you see any Uyghur faces? Do you see any Tibetan separatists? Do you see any Arabic people wearing unusual clothes? Do you see any Africans like the ones that hang about Guangdong, where unethical business dealings often occur? Do you see any CIA-funded Hong Kongers plotting to destroy the motherland? You breathe a sigh of relief – you don't see any sign of trouble.

Many of your fellow passengers have Qinese faces. After all, you are in Qina, going to America. You are not the only one. There are others like you who are making the journey. Who are these people? No doubt they are wealthy, like Mark must be. No doubt they are successful businessmen, scholars, engineers, doctors, lawyers, the "cream of the crop." Now you are one of them. How lucky you are!

"Hold my hand," you say, reaching and intertwining your fingers with Mark's.

The whole plane around you shakes. The floor, the walls, the overhead bins that store the luggage, it's all shuddering like you are in the belly of a dragon. The airplane is taking off. Don't be frightened, dear Little Comrade. The humming noise you hear is well within normal parameters.

Look out the window, what do you see? The ground is passing by so quickly. Almost as fast as the high-speed train. As the plane lifts off, you feel a sensation in the pit of your stomach. Your grip on Mark's hand tightens. The airplane lurches upwards, dips down, and up and up again. You feel it in your stomach like you are in a roller coaster.

"My ears hurt."

"Oh?" he says. "That usually happens when the plane is landing, but it can happen during takeoff too. Try this." He pinches your nostrils closed. "Now try to blow air out of your nose." You do as he instructs. Your cheeks fill up with air. Then, almost like magic, you hear a pop in your ears and it feels better.

"Chew on this gum," Mark says. "Some people find that it helps."

You take a stick of gum from him and put it into your mouth. How does that feel, dear Little Comrade?

By now the plane has levelled out. Would it surprise you to know that you are now thirty thousand feet above the ground? How does it feel? If you get sick in the stomach, there is a paper bag in the magazine pouch in front of you.

Time passes slowly. Your nervousness has now given way to restlessness, sore back muscles, sore shoulders and neck pain. It is not so different from sitting on a train, is it? Granted, the service is a little better, but you don't care about such things. What concerns you mostly is the price. Presently, the air stewardess comes down the aisle with a pushcart containing complimentary drinks.

The tall blond stewardess is standing there, one hand on the back of your chair. She leans slightly forward in a trained, airline stewardess manner, offering you a drink from her selection. You hesitate, unsure of how to answer.

Mark steps in and orders a cup of apple juice. The stewardess hands him a tiny, expensive-looking bottle of wine. You are thirsty, but the food on the train always costs so much. Even though you have been Mark's girlfriend for a while now, you are still true to your old self.

"Go on, it's free," Mark says.

You shake your head. You wave your hand in front of your face, pursing your lips as you do so. "No need," you say. There is no such thing as a free lunch. These tricksters will find some way to charge you for the drink, obviously.

The stewardess smiles in a friendly, non-judgmental way. She continues to the passenger behind you. You lick your lips and swallow. Your mouth is dry.

You have so many questions you want to ask Mark. He's talked to you already so much about what to expect. But for some reason it seems like you cannot remember any of it.

"Do they have Qinese food in America?" you ask. "I don't want to eat that nasty foreign food."

When you didn't have the chance to go abroad you deliberately sought out exotic foods like sushi. But now that the real deal is going down, you find that your loyalties, your tastes, your whole person is inescapably Qinese. Strange, isn't it?

"Don't worry, my sisters will cook delicious Qinese food for you," Mark says.

"Too bad your family isn't from Sichuan. I like spicy food," you say.

"I have a sister from Sichuan. She's a good cook. She'll prepare some food for you."

"Really? You're full of surprises. I'm excited."

The prospect of eating Mark's sister's Sichuan dishes is something tangible you can look forward to. It's an absolute, achievable goal that you know will happen. The rest of America remains an abstract, uncertain idea that frightens you, even as you fly there.

With this new sense of security and self-confidence, you think to yourself, If only my parents, and my younger brother, and Bo Bo could see me now.

"Wait till I tell my mom I've been to America. She won't believe me," you say.

"You can buy her a souvenir. Then she'll have to believe you."

"My mom and brother thought I was joking when I told them I was planning a trip to America. But my dad didn't. He got angry. He said I'm betraying my country. He was so disappointed."

"Why? That's stupid."

"No. He's right. I love Qina; the government helped us villagers so much, built up the country from nothing."

"You'll like America, it's even better."

A rhythm is established on the plane. It's a sort of "de facto" schedule that everyone abides by. Drinks are served. Then there is something to eat. A period of rest follows.

You watch movies on the screen in front of you. The cabin lights dim. You fall asleep. When you wake up you find the blond stewardess standing at your side.

"Chicken or beef?" she says.

The words are spoken in English and you do not understand. She repeats herself, this time in Qinese. "Ghee? Neew Row?" These are the only two Qinese words she knows.

You realize what she has said. You remember this English word, which sounds familiar to you. "Chee-kaan," you manage to say, pronouncing your word in tortured English.

It's easy for you. The first part sounds like *Qi*, which means life force energy. And the last part sounds like *Kan*, which means *to look*. Qi-Kan. Chicken.

Well done, Little Comrade! All those English lessons taught by your Qinese teachers in middle school and high school have not gone to waste. It is all coming back to you. Show this foreigner that you are just as capable of learning a foreign language as she is, and that she is no better than you are. She may have blond hair, she may be a foot taller than you are, she may be a native speaker of that ever so lucrative language, English, but when it comes down to sheer brain matter, "pound for pound, catty for catty," you are just as smart as she is.

You must remember, dear Little Comrade, the outside world is not like Qina. In Qina, apart from the metropolises, your neighbours, friends, co-workers, almost everyone you see on the bus, on the street, in the shopping mall and elsewhere, is Qinese. The harmonious society you are used to will soon be replaced by one plagued by contradiction, jealousy, tension and chaos.

Be on your toes. You are already flying over the Pacific, well outside of Qinese airspace. You are no longer in Qina. From now on, your life will be a series of these micro confrontations, these little battles of ego, these little skirmishes of nationality. Will you assert yourself in each of these situations and represent your country, Qina, responsibly? Will you do justice to your fellow people, to your heritage? This is a question you will have to ask yourself every day when you look in the mirror in the morning. Are you up for it? Make no mistake, over time it will become tiring, it will become tedious, but nevertheless this is a duty you must never fail to do. Wherever you go you will be the sole representative of what people think of Qina. Whether you like it or not that is how people will perceive you.

# XLII. ADAPT
# WHEN NECESSARY

Mark nudges you awake.

The plane is making its final descent. Look out the window. What do you see?

A clear, dark, beautiful night sky. The city's lights, like ten thousand sparkling candles, dot the ground. It is an incredible sight. It is a city called New York, the biggest city in this fantasy country you have been dreaming about for so long, "America." For you, it is the prize, the crown jewel of the whole world.

Your heart leaps up into your throat as the plane descends. After many, many hours, a seemingly endless flight, the plane touches down with a violent jolt.

It rolls and rolls across the tarmac until it reaches its destination gate at the terminal. The passengers are already out of their seats, getting their baggage from the overhead compartments.

You stretch and yawn. You slept well on the flight. The comfortable chair and Mark's warm hand served their purpose. It is evening now. Congratulations, you made it to "America."

Soon, following crowds of people, you are out of the airport. The air is so fresh. But, really, is it so different from a Shanghai night sky? Perhaps. But never mind. Follow Mark. See where he takes you.

Two women are waiting for him. Both are Qinese faced, but one is young while the other is older with clever eyes.

"There's my sister and aunt," Mark says.

The sister's name is Su. Su looks much like you do. Thin, pretty, but better dressed, more fashionable clothes. Mark doesn't tell you his aunt's name, so you just call her Aunty.

They are waiting by a car. You are so lucky. You are part of the civilized world, where everyone has a nice car.

Mark gets behind the wheel. Aunty sits in the passenger seat beside him, while you and Su sit in the back. As Mark drives, look out the window.

You see the streets of the city. You go along the highway and see houses pass by. You see tall, sleek apartment buildings. Even though it is dark, everything looks so clean, so nice and calm.

One thing you notice right away. There's so much empty space in this foreign country. It's strange, as if people put buildings so far apart, like they want to take up more space. It makes no sense to you. The roads, the houses, the buildings, the trees, the parks, everything is so far apart. How do people walk anywhere? But, of course, they don't need to walk, since they have cars.

As you look around, ask yourself, have you been here before? No, of course not. And yet, oddly enough, it all looks familiar. Maybe you are imagining things. Maybe in another life you have seen what you are seeing now for the first time.

Throughout the car ride Mark and Aunty chat in a dialect you don't understand. They seem to have much to say to each other, but their voices are subdued and serious. You and Su remain mostly silent. Su only answers when she is spoken to.

"Do you want something to eat?" asks Mark.

"No," you say, politely shaking your head.

You just met Su and Aunty; you don't want them to think you are greedy. But neither seems to hear you. Su, like you, is looking out the window.

Mark stops at a fast-food restaurant. He explains that Aunty is hungry and wants to get something called a taco, a kind of strange sandwich from Mexico. He also needs to use the toilet. He and Aunty exit the vehicle, leaving you and Su alone.

There's an uncomfortable silence. You want Su to like you, so you make some chitchat. "You speak Putonghua so well," you say. "How long have you been here?"

"Two years," says Su, so quietly you would not be able to hear her but for the silence in the car.

"How did you come here?" you ask.

"Mark brought me, what else?" she says. She doesn't sound entirely friendly.

"It must be nice to have family here."

She lets out a grunt. "Yeah, right," she says.

"Aren't you his sister?"

"Sure, isn't that what he told you?"

"How many brothers and sisters are here in your family?"

"It depends, some come and go. Know what I mean? You're my sister now, aren't you?"

"Yeah, I guess I am. I heard you have a sister from Sichuan province who can cook real spicy dishes."

"Who's that?"

"I don't know her name. Mark told me. Don't you know her?"

"From Sichuan? Maybe that was Little Tang. But she left a while ago."

"Left? Where to?"

"Who knows. Aunty got rid of her."

You don't quite understand what Su is saying. It doesn't sound like what you expected. You sit in silence, not knowing what else to say.

"How's your English?" you ask, after some time.

Su shrugs. "I didn't really know any before I came here. Actually, I haven't learned much more since coming here."

"No? How is that possible? Doesn't everyone speak English here?"

"All the sisters speak Qinese. We don't go out much. We speak English to the customers, I guess. But you know, it's just silly talk. You can't learn much from that. And if they want to talk, mostly they just want you to listen."

"I see. So, I guess I'll be working too then?" you say.

"Sure, you're pretty. Isn't that why Mark brought you over?"

"Yeah, I guess so. What exactly is the job?"

"Why don't you wait for Aunty to explain that to you."

Mark comes back with a bag of food. You want to ask him and Aunty about your new job. But for some reason it doesn't feel right to ask them at that moment, with Su sitting there. Something feels funny, like nobody wants to talk about it.

The food smells delicious. "Here, you said you didn't want any, but I got you one anyway," says Aunty. Aunty hands you the paper bag. After refusing politely, you reach in and take out a wrapped sandwich, thanking her profusely as you do so. It is hot at least. Bite into it. Your first meal in "America." It's crispy. It is beef morsels in a cornbread shell called a tortilla, with some lettuce and tomato and white sauce. To your surprise, it tastes very good. Aunty is so thoughtful. All your worries were for nothing. You think you really may enjoy living here.

You eat in the back seat. When you look out the window again, Mark is pulling into an empty strip mall. He parks the car in front of an electronics store that sells computer parts. Beside this is another shop with a blackened window featuring an electric neon sign. You cannot read the words because they are in English. The writing says, "Asian Beauty Massage Parlour and Spa."

"You can sleep here," says Mark.

"Aren't we going to be living together?" you ask him.

"Yeah, of course. But my place isn't big enough. For now, you can live here with Aunty and Su and the other sisters, okay? Besides, it's convenient for you. You'll be able to work a lot and make more money. Just until we make other arrangements. Come on, let's get out of the car. You'll like it."

Su has gone ahead inside. Aunty puts her hand on your elbow, making clicking sounds with her tongue, ushering you in. She has your luggage in hand, which is only one small case, but she's carrying it for you.

"So what's the job?" you say. "Are you sure I can do it?" You were asking Mark, but Aunty steers you away from him, and answers.

"Of course," she says, "it's just massages. You know, anyone can do it. It's simple."

"Oh," you say. You didn't really know what to expect. But now that Aunty says it, it seems like the right job, the only job that you can do. Still, you can't help but feel a little disappointed.

What were you expecting, dear Little Comrade, a job as a stockbroker?

"I don't really know how to give massages. And I'm not very strong, my hands are weak," you say.

"It's okay," says Aunty. "You don't need to be strong. You don't need a lot of muscle, it's all in the technique. I'll show you how to do it tomorrow. But tonight, why don't you unpack and go to sleep."

"But where's Mark going? Isn't he going to stay with us here?"

"No," Mark says, "I need to go take care of some things and see some relatives. I'll see you tomorrow. Aunty will take care of you, don't worry."

You are sad to see Mark drive off in his car, but there is nothing you can do.

Inside the shopfront is an empty waiting area. Your sisters are working in the backrooms, which you cannot see. Aunty introduces you to them. There is Lotus from Guangdong, and Cecilia from Hunan, May-Tong from Fujian and Su from Anhui.

Aunty leads you down some stairs in the back, to a basement area that has a small room with some bunks. The air is very stale. The state of the place is squalid. It looks worse than the bunk in the factory dormitory.

"Here, you go to sleep. Tomorrow, we'll get you set up," says Aunty. "I have to go take care of the front desk now, there's lots of work to do. Good night."

# XLIII. ACCEPT YOUR COUNTRY

So begins the wonderful life in "America" that you always dreamed of.

Over the next few weeks you perform your duties as Aunty has instructed and taught you to do. This involves, for the most part, disrobing each customer and stimulating him until he is satisfied with your efforts.

Needless to say, the customers are always male.

For the first few days the novelty of seeing all these different men makes your life somewhat interesting. Some of these men are handsome. Some have white, pink or tanned skin, green eyes, blue eyes. But for the most part they are a scrappy-looking bunch. Quite a few of the customers have Qinese faces, and if they are not Qinese they are Asian. People with other skin colours are common too, like brown or black. You don't know where these people are from, but many of them speak English to you. Slowly you begin to understand more of what they say to you. Their English is not always so good. If you spoke more to them your English would be almost as good as theirs.

Regardless of what the men look like, there is one thing they want in common. Fortunately, it is a task that, after your experience with Q, and your steep learning curve with Mark, you are quite capable of. Aunty is also able to help you with any questions you may have, though you are too embarrassed to ask her. Su seems to have taken a liking to you or at least she is not as unfriendly as she was the first night when she came to pick you up at the airport.

To your disappointment, however, Mark has little time for you. Every night he is away with his "relatives." You are stuck in the shop, to live in the bunk. You miss his company, but you say nothing to Aunty or your sisters. Besides, you have to keep busy working.

All the food you eat is delivered to the shop. Sitting in the lounge, you eat with your coworkers, in front of a television.

On the news are reports of violence. A maniac with a gun has killed many women, women just like you, working in a spa just like yours. It's awful. It's only one of a few mass killings that have happened recently.

Outside the glass doors of the shop, a man with a baseball cap bangs on the window and spits in your direction. The man shouts slurs and obscenities, and vows to return later in the evening.

Once a week, or once every two weeks, you go out, accompanied by Aunty and one or two of the sisters.

On the streets, you see homeless people huddled in sleeping bags, under cardboard boxes, broken needles lying around. Once, a group of white men and women throw empty beer cans at you from a passing car. A group of teenagers, rowdy and violent looking, shove you and grab you by the arm. They trip you and call you bad names, while laughing.

Another time, you witness a large riot – some people looting stores, and other people throwing rocks and setting things on fire. It's all confusing, bizarre and frightening. These experiences make you unhappy and want to hide indoors.

After you have settled into your routine, you realize that your visa is expired. The date that you were supposed to leave has already elapsed. Mark is nowhere to be seen. You're not sure, but you think there has to be some kind of mistake.

You find Aunty in the lounge room, eating some instant noodles. "I haven't seen Mark for the last few weeks. Do you know where he is?" you ask.

"He's gone, he had some business to do, back in Qina." The news hurts. He did not even say goodbye to you. Aunty sees this in your pained expression. "Don't worry, he'll be back eventually," she says. "You sure fell hard for him, didn't you?"

You say nothing. Sit down and watch the TV that is playing in the lounge. What more can you do? You must make money to pay back all the expenses you incurred coming over here. You are not sure exactly how much the expenses were, but obviously it was very expensive. It may take you some time to pay back the debt that you owe.

Besides, you cannot leave because your visa is expired and you are in this strange and unfamiliar country illegally. Who knows what will happen to you if you are discovered by the authorities. They may throw you in jail, lock you away forever.

Aunty warns you to never tell anyone about your visa problems or someone is likely to report you. Who would you tell, anyway? The customers who visit you are always different. You cannot trust them. For the most part they don't even speak your language, and the ones that do are obviously very suspect people otherwise they wouldn't be there asking you to do the things you do.

Truth be told, the things that you accept being done to your body, and which you allow your body to do, become less and less of a concern to you.

Tonight a man comes to visit. He has come many times before, and he has developed a fondness for you in particular. Each time he gets closer to his goal, which is to persuade you to do something with him which your sisters have also, without saying so out loud, quietly encouraged you to do. You don't want to, and yet, it seems pointless now to resist. Mark is not there, and even if he were, you somehow know that he would be in support of it.

And so you lie back, you let the man do as he pleases. It will earn you some extra money. This sets a precedent for all the customers that come after who make this request. For the following months, you are indifferent to what happens.

One day you show Aunty something that has been bothering you for a while now. She takes one look and sends you with Su to see a doctor and to get an anonymous test done.

When you bring the test results back, Aunty looks at it and immediately shoos you out of the room.

This may be hard for you to accept, but you are diseased, Little Comrade. You have a terrible disease. Aunty cannot even say the name of it aloud. Soon you will die. There is no cure for AIDS. There is no point in seeing a doctor, you cannot afford it, and anyway doctors frighten you.

Aunty is kind enough to give you some money. Or maybe it is because she just wants you to leave, the sooner the better. She puts the money in an envelope and leaves it outside the door of the shop, afraid to touch you. After you leave, they put on plastic gloves and throw out your mattress and any other items near your bed.

You open the envelope and take the bills out. It's not much, but it will last you a few days on the streets, on your own.

In time you wander down to a waterfront. Where can you go? There's no point in trying to find anyone now, not Mark, not Steve. So far from home. You sit down on a bench and look out across the waves. Listen to the sound of the water. Is this the ocean, you wonder. You wonder if Qina is on the other side. You know that that is where you belong, and that you should never have left.

You take out your phone. You have kept the same phone all this time, with its cracked screen. The phone card does not work here, obviously, in this foreign country, but you find your mother's phone number anyway. You type a message to her anyway. A tear falls onto the screen and you wipe it off. It is the last message you will send. You do not sign it; she will know who it is from.

Mama, I'm sorry for everything. I am very sick. I will die soon. I miss you.

Close your eyes, Little Comrade. What do you see?
You are Qinese, you realize. You will never leave Qina.

Thank you for reading *Letters to Little Comrade: A Guide for Girls*. This pamphlet is produced by the Qinese Bureau of Public Affairs. Please send all correspondence and fan mail to the address below:

Qinese Bureau of Public Affairs
Beijing 102200
No. 3 Renmin Lu, West Plaza Street
People's Republic of Qina

# ACKNOWLEDGEMENTS

On behalf of the author the Qinese Bureau of Public Affairs thanks:

His partner, Liu Wan, for keeping the home tidy, cooking dinner and performing the necessary functions incumbent of a wife.

His daughter, for her good temper, reverence and filial piety.

His mother and father, for exhorting him to study hard and become an exemplary citizen.

His brothers, for setting examples in childhood and adulthood.

His nieces and nephews, for their obedience and studiousness.

His Canadian publishers and editors – Noelle, Paul, Ashley and Jennifer – for their faith and devotion to the fatherland.

His intellectual mentor and friend Mr. Maloney

His model high school teacher, Linda Wolsley, who served the greater good.

His respected acquaintance Dr. Erika Loic, for her self-effacing personality and academic exertions.

And a special thanks to the Qinese Bureau of Public Affairs for making this book possible.

Dan K. Woo's family came to Canada in the 1970s. His grandfather was a fire captain and the first firefighter to die on duty in British Hong Kong, partly a result of the British colonial system. In 2018, Woo won the Ken Klonsky Award for *Learning How to Love China* (Quattro Books). His writing has appeared in such publications as the *South China Morning Post*, *Quill & Quire*, *China Daily USA* and elsewhere. A Toronto native, he lives with his partner in the city and writes in his free time.